BEST MAN
AND THE
RUNAWAY BRIDE

BEST MAN
AND THE
RUNAWAY BRIDE

KANDY SHEPHERD

MILLS & BOON

First published in Great Britain 2018
by Mills & Boon, an imprint of HarperCollins*Publishers*
1 London Bridge Street, London, SE1 9GF

Large Print edition 2018

© 2018 Kandy Shepherd

ISBN: 978-0-263-07439-0

MIX
Paper from
responsible sources
FSC™ C007454

This book is produced from independently certified
FSC™ paper to ensure responsible forest management.
For more information visit www.harpercollins.co.uk/green.

Printed and bound in Great Britain
by CPI Group (UK) Ltd, Croydon, CR0 4YY

In memory of my dear friend
Patrick J Houston, married to his soulmate,
my friend Louise, for more than
forty years after proposing to her on
their second date. Charismatic, big-hearted
and very handsome, he was truly
a real-life romance hero.

CHAPTER ONE

WHERE WAS THE BRIDE? She should have been at the church a half-hour ago. Max Conway paced back and forth on the pavement in front of the historic sandstone building. As best man at the wedding, he'd been despatched outside to report on the bride's arrival status. Again, he glanced down at his watch. Traditionally a bride was tardy but this much late was ridiculous. No wonder the groom, standing inside all by himself at the altar, was grim-faced and tapping his foot.

Organ music drifted out through the arched windows of the church. The notes had a trill of desperation as the organist started her wedding repertoire for the third time. Anticipation levels inside would be rising as the congregation waited—and waited.

Max checked the traffic app on his phone to

see if there were problems. All roads leading to the church in Sydney's posh eastern suburbs were clear. The bridesmaids had arrived without any problem. *But still no bride.* He was about to turn on his heel and go back inside to give the glowering groom an update—a task he didn't relish—when the bridal car approached. His shoulders sagged with relief. *She was here.*

Through the tinted window of the luxury limousine he could see a froth of white veil framing a lovely female face. Nikki Lucas. Max recognised her straight away, though he'd only met her for the first time at the rehearsal two nights before. Honey-blonde hair. Soft brown eyes. Tall and slender. A truly beautiful bride. Well worth the wait for the lucky groom.

At the rehearsal she'd greeted Max with a smile so dazzling he'd been momentarily stunned. She'd been warm and welcoming to her fiancé's best man—a total stranger to her. If she'd realised who he was—who he had once been—she'd been too well-mannered to mention it. The rehearsal had gone smoothly and he'd got the impression Ms Lucas was efficient and organised. Not the kind of woman to be so late for her own wedding.

The wealthy father of the bride sat next to her in the back seat. Why hadn't he hurried his daughter along? Max found such lack of punctuality unpardonable. What was Ms Lucas's game? If this were his bride—not that he had any intention of marrying any time soon—he would be furious. The limo slowed to a halt. No doubt he'd be greeted with a flurry of excuses. He would cut her short, bustle her inside and get this tardy bride up the aisle pronto.

He ran to the bride's door and yanked it open. 'You're here,' he said through gritted teeth, swallowing the *where the hell have you been.*

He didn't get so much as a smile in response. In fact the errant bride looked downright hostile. Her face was as pale as the layers of tulle that framed it, her mouth set tight. She swung her long, elegant legs out of the car, shook off the hand he offered her to help, and stood up in a flurry of fluffy white skirts.

She gave no apologies, no explanations, no excuses. Just a tersely spoken command. 'You have to get me out of here.'

Max stared at her. 'Get you up the aisle, you mean,' he said. 'You're late. There's a church full of guests waiting for you. Not to mention your groom.'

'Him.' She shook her head so vehemently her long veil whipped around her face. 'I'm not going to marry that man. I thought I could go through with it but I can't.'

By now her father had clambered out of the car to join them. The limo took off with a squeal of tyres, the driver muttering he was late for his next job.

'Think about this, sweetheart,' said the older man. He handed her the bouquet of white roses that she had left behind her on the car seat. 'You can't just walk out on your wedding.'

'Yes, I can. You can't talk me out of this, Dad. If you won't help me, Max here will.' She spat out his name as if it were a dirty word. 'It's the least he can do as best man to the creep who convinced me to marry him under false pretences.'

She glared at Max through narrowed eyes. 'That is, unless you're just as much lying pond scum as he is.'

Max wasn't usually lost for words. But the insult came from nowhere. Where was the smiling charmer from the rehearsal? Behind the perfect make-up the bride was grim-faced and steely eyed. 'I don't consider myself to be pond scum,' Max said through gritted teeth. 'But my duty as best man is to get you into the church for your wedding.'

'There isn't going to be a wedding. Your duty as a decent human being is to help me get away from here. Now.' Her hands shook with agitation and she kept looking anxiously towards the church.

Max's first reaction was to back away from the bride. He wasn't good with crazy. This was something more than pre-wedding nerves. There was no trace of the joyous, vibrant woman he'd met at the rehearsal. But then her lush pink mouth trembled and her eyes clouded with something he couldn't quite place—fear, anxiety, disappointment? It made him swallow a retort. How well did he actually know the groom? He'd played tennis with him back in high school but had only reconnected with him just weeks before the wedding—had been surprised to be asked to be best man. The groom could well be pond scum these days for all he knew. But he'd made a commitment to be best man. That made him Team Groom.

The father took her arm. 'Now, Nikki, there's no need to—'

The bride turned on her father with a swirl of white skirts, glaring back at Max as she did so. 'I'm sorry, Dad,' she said, her voice unsteady. 'I can't do it.'

She indicated the church with a wave of a perfectly manicured hand. Her large diamond engagement ring flashed in the afternoon summer sunlight. 'Please tell everyone to party on without me. Don't let all that food and wine go to waste.' Her mouth curled. 'Maybe someone could have the fun of smashing Alan's lying, scheming face into the wedding cake—all three tiers of it.'

'Maybe not,' Max said, trying not to let a smile twitch at the corners of his mouth at the thought of the somewhat supercilious groom facedown in the frosting.

He made his voice calm and reassuring. 'I know you must be nervous.'

Pre-performance nerves. He knew all about them. There was nothing more nerve-wracking than stepping out onto the centre court at Wimbledon with the world watching him defend his title.

'Nervous?' Her cheeks flushed and her eyes glittered. 'I'm not nervous. I'm mad as hell.' She brandished the cascade of white roses as if it were a weapon. Max ducked. 'The wedding is cancelled.'

'Why?' At the rehearsal she'd seemed to be floating on a cloud of happiness. For one long, secret moment he had envied her groom his gorgeous, vivacious bride-to-be. Despite his success at the highest rank of his chosen sport, and all the female attention that came with it, at age thirty Max was still single.

'You want a reason?' She raised her perfectly shaped brows. 'How about four reasons? His two ex-wives and two children.'

Max frowned. 'You knew Alan was divorced.'

'Divorced *once*. With no children. He lied.' Her voice ended on a heart-rending whimper. 'One of the reasons I fell for him was that he told me he was longing for children. Like…like I was.' Her face seemed to crumple; all the poise Max had admired melted away to leave only wide-eyed bewilderment.

'How did you find out?' he asked.

'His first ex-wife called to warn me off Alan. Didn't want to see me get fooled and hurt by him like she had been. He called her a vindictive witch. Then the second ex-wife wife called to tell me about their three-year-old twin sons and how he'd deserted them. Oh, and warned me he was on the verge of bankruptcy now that he'd gone through all her money.'

Max gasped. The dad hissed. Nikki was a successful businesswoman. Being both beautiful and wealthy made her quite the catch—and vulnerable to a fortune hunter.

'You believed her?' said Max.

She shook her head. 'I trusted my fiancé. But

I had her investigated. Definitive proof she was telling the truth came just as I waved off my bridesmaids and was about to get into the limo.' Her breath caught on a hitch, dangerously close to a sob. 'I can't marry a liar and a fraud.'

'Go in there and tell him that,' said Max.

'I couldn't bear the humiliation.' She looked up at him, her eyes pleading now. 'You know all about humiliation.'

Max grimaced. Of course he did. Evidence of his disastrous final game where he'd injured his elbow so badly still circulated on the Internet: the thrown racket, his writhing in pain on the grass court surface of Wimbledon. People had even made memes of it.

'Yes,' he said through gritted teeth, not appreciating the reminder.

'Please help me get away. I can't run down the street to hail a cab dressed like this.'

Tears glistened in her brown eyes, making them luminous. Max had a weakness for female tears. But he was also a man of his word. He was the best man. An honourable position with duties he took seriously. It would take more than tears to recruit him to Team Bride. As she looked up at him, a single teardrop rolled slowly down her cheek. He had to fight an impulse to wipe it gently away with his thumb. *She was another man's bride.* She sniffed and her voice quivered as she spoke. 'You say you're not pond scum, now prove it to me.'

Nikki held her breath as she looked up at Max Conway for his answer. She hadn't expected to find him standing guard outside the church, ready to corral her inside. In fact, she hardly knew the guy. Just was aware he was a celebrity athlete and had a well-publicised love life.

The first she'd known that her groom's best man was the world's golden boy of tennis—featured in countless 'sexiest men alive' media round-ups—was when she'd met him at the rehearsal. Just another of her former fiancé's secrets, she thought with a twist of bitterness.

She could read the struggle on Max's face—with his spiky light brown hair and blue eyes, he was every bit as handsome as his photos. Duty warred an obvious battle with gentlemanly instincts to help a bride in distress. The media did not consider him a gentleman. She didn't care. All she wanted was his help to get away. The clock was ticking. Her father had reluctantly gone to tell everyone that the bride would be a no-show. If she was going to escape, she'd have to do it now.

'Are you quite sure you want to do this?' Max said.

'Yes, yes, yes,' she said, unable to keep the impatience from her voice. At any moment Alan might come raging outside. She shuddered at the thought.

'There'll be no going back. It's Alan who'll be humiliated.'

'*Huh!* Finding out the truth about him from his ex-wives rates high in humiliation. Being foolish enough to have believed his lies even higher.'

She clutched Max by the sleeve of his dark best-man suit. Looked with trepidation across to the Gothic-style arched wooden doors that led to the interior of the church. People were beginning to spill out down the steps. Ahead of the pack was the wedding photographer, brandishing his camera aimed at her. Forget Max. She gathered up her skirts. Got ready to run. Risked a final glance up at him. 'Are you going to help me or not?'

'I don't like liars.'

'Is that a "yes"?'

In reply he took her by the arm. Through the sheer fabric of her sleeve she could feel the warmth and strength of his grip. 'My car is around the corner. We'll have to run.'

She started to run but only got a few steps before she stumbled. The combination of bumpy pavement, long skirts and high, skinny heels wasn't conducive to a speedy escape.

'Ditch the shoes,' he said tersely. She kicked them off. One after the other they flew into the air and landed side down on the pavement. 'And the flowers.' The white flowers landed near the white shoes with a flurry of petals, forming a tableau of lost dreams on the grey of the tarmac. She didn't look back.

They had rounded the corner from the church

when she heard the first shout. More outraged bellow than civilised protest. She cringed at the anger in Alan's voice. Max's grip on her arm tightened as he hurried her along. 'We're not going fast enough,' he said.

She wished she could tear away her long skirts. 'I'm moving as fast as I—'

Her protest ended in a gasp as he effortlessly swept her up to cradle her in his arms. 'Hold on tight,' he said as he broke into a run—at twice her speed.

Max Conway was a tall, powerfully built man famed for the relentless power of his serve. Instinctively Nikki looped her arms around his neck and pressed herself close against a solid wall of muscle.

'You…you don't have to carry me,' she managed to choke out.

'I do,' he said. She noticed he wasn't the slightest bit out of breath even while running at full stride weighed down by the burden of a bride. 'That is, if you really want to escape from your groom.'

The edge to his voice made her stiffen in his

arms. Did he think this was some kind of attention-seeking ruse? That she would let Alan catch her and lead her triumphantly back to the wedding? She went to retort but realised he didn't know her any better than she knew him. She would never behave like that. But he wasn't to know.

It seemed like only seconds before he stopped by a modest sedan parked by the kerb. Wouldn't a sports celebrity like Max Conway drive something flashier? Unless he wanted to stay under the radar for some reason. In this case, it would serve her well if Alan tried to follow her. Once in the traffic, this car would be anonymous.

Max put her down by the passenger door. The pavement was warm to her stockinged feet. She was in a wedding dress and no shoes. It made her feel vulnerable and aware of her predicament. For the first time she questioned the wisdom of begging a stranger to take her away. But there was something about Max's assured, take-charge attitude that made her feel she could trust him.

He unlocked the car with a fob on his key ring

and held open her door. 'Jump in,' he said. 'And be quick.'

That was easier said than done with a voluminous full skirt to tuck in around her. With fumbling fingers, she'd just managed to fasten her seat belt when the car took off with a jolt and a screech of tyres. 'We've got company,' Max said by way of explanation.

Nikki glanced behind her to see what he meant. Heading towards the car was a red-faced Alan, followed closely by her sister, resplendent in her bridesmaid's dress, her sweet face screwed up in anguish. The wedding photographer followed— snapping gleefully away at the runaway bride. Nikki's heart started to race and she choked on her breath. For the first time, she realised the enormity of what she had done. How it would affect so many people other than herself. She hadn't even told her beloved sister.

But she'd make it up to them later. Far better to offend a few people than to chain herself in marriage to the wrong man. 'Step on it,' she urged Max.

It wasn't long before they'd reached her older

style waterfront apartment in Double Bay. She'd bought it with her first big profits from her business.

Max pulled into the driveway. 'Have you got keys?'

'No need. The entry is security coded.'

She expected him to bundle her out into the courtyard and speed off. Instead, he got out of the car to come around and open the passenger door for her. She realised Alan had never done that. Not once. Why had she let herself be so swept off her feet by him?

'Ouch!' The gravelled courtyard was not kind to stockinged feet. She started to pick her way across it, wincing as she went.

'Allow me,' Max said. Before she could protest she was swept up into his arms again as he carried her across the courtyard to the front door.

'This is very chivalrous of you,' she said, flushing.

'Nothing is chivalrous about the best man running off with the bride,' he said with a wry twist to his mouth that didn't quite pass as a smile.

'But the bride is very grateful,' she said. 'More grateful than she can say.'

He continued to hold her as she coded in her password. Then kicked the door open and carried her inside. It was as if he were carrying her over the threshold like a *real* bride on her wedding night. The thought was way too disconcerting. She struggled to be put down. He immediately set her back on her feet. She fussed with her dress to cover her confusion.

'What now for you?' he asked.

'I intend to barricade myself in my apartment.'

'And then?'

'I have a plan.' She didn't really. The plan had been to spend the night with her new husband— she shuddered at even the thought of it—in a luxury city hotel then next day set off to a honeymoon in an even more expensive hotel in Dubai. Alan's choice. 'But I'm not going to tell you about it. Then you can truthfully tell people you don't know where I am.'

'You mean Alan?'

She nodded. 'I really and truly don't want him

to find me. And I don't want to make things more awkward for you than I already have.'

'I get that,' he said.

'Just one more thing.' She tugged the diamond engagement ring—that she had worn with such optimism for the future—off her finger. 'Can you give this to him, please? I have no further use for it.'

'Like a best man's duty in reverse.'

He took the ring from her, his warm fingers brushing against hers as he did so. She snatched her hand back, not welcoming the tingle of aware- ness that shot through her. She'd been about to wed another man, for heaven's sake. How could she feel such a flutter of attraction to his best man? Especially a guy who had cheated on his tennis-player girlfriend—a woman as famous as he was—and been involved in a highly pub- licised paternity dispute.

An awkward silence fell between them. She shifted from one stockinged foot to another, not wanting to meet his gaze. 'Thank you for helping me,' she said finally. 'It was very good of you.'

'Good doesn't come into it. I'm not proud of

myself for helping you run away. I went against my principles. I'm not convinced it was the right thing for you to do either. I seriously hope you don't regret it.'

The full impact of what she'd done might not hit her until Max left her alone in her apartment, surrounded by the disarray of her wedding preparations and honeymoon packing. But he didn't need to sound self-righteous about it. It wasn't for Max Conway to sit in judgement against her. Grateful though she was for his help.

Anger flooded through her. 'There's one more thing you don't know about your friend Alan. After his twins, he had a vasectomy so he couldn't have more children. The man who used to toss names for our future kids around with me. Spent hours discussing what colour eyes they might have. Was he ever going to tell me he was shooting blanks? Or let me go through fertility treatment when I didn't fall pregnant?'

'I have no words,' Max said, tight-lipped. No criticism of his friend, of course. Not when the famous tennis player himself had cheated and lied.

'I'll never regret walking out on that despicable excuse for a man. But letting my family and friends down? Not doing due diligence on the man before I agreed to marry him? I suspect I'll always regret my lapse in judgement. I wouldn't have done a minor business deal without all the facts, yet I was prepared to commit my life to a person I didn't really know. I wanted that life so much…the husband and kids.'

'I can only wish you good luck in whatever you end up doing,' he said. Looking serious suited him and it struck her again how good-looking he was. No wonder the public was so fascinated by him.

'What I don't regret is putting my trust in you to help me,' she said. Max might be pond scum in his personal life and be friend to a cheating, lying fraud. But he had come through for her. That was all that counted.

On impulse she leaned up and kissed him on his smooth, tanned cheek. She was stunned by the sensation that shot through her at the contact, brief as it was. He didn't kiss her back. Why would he? She'd just run out on his friend. 'I won't say I'll return the favour for you some day because it's not the kind of favour you want to call on, is it?'

He half smiled at that and turned to leave. She watched him as he strode back to his car, broad-shouldered and athletic. Unless she glimpsed him on television, slamming a tennis ball at his opponent in some top-level tournament, she would never see Max Conway again.

CHAPTER TWO

Six months later

MAX HADN'T COME to the small Indonesian island of Nusa Lembongan for fun. On previous visits to nearby Bali he had stayed with friends in luxurious private villas the size of mansions, with all their needs and whims catered to by a team of attendants devoted purely to their comfort. Near the beach in fashionable Seminyak. Overlooking the sea on a cliff top in exclusive Uluwatu. High in the treetops of Ubud.

Not this time.

The last six months had been hell. Everything that could have gone wrong had gone wrong in both his professional and personal life. He had come to this small island, off the east coast of the main island of Bali, on his own. Not to party. But to make plans to reinvent himself.

Yesterday he had checked in to the Big Blue Bungalows, a small family-run hotel on the beach at Frangipani Bay on the south-west end of the island. He'd come with just a backpack and his laptop. The accommodation wasn't backpacker basic, nor was it the five-star luxury he was accustomed to. Built as a collection of traditional-style bungalows and small villas with thatched roofs, the hotel was comfortable without being overly luxurious—and not without its own rustic charm.

Lembongan was much quieter and less touristy than Bali, with more scooters and bicycles and few cars on the narrow streets. He hadn't been there twenty-four hours and he'd already cycled halfway around the island on a pushbike he'd borrowed from the hotel. The friend who'd recommended the island had warned Max he might get bored after a few days. Max doubted that. He just wanted to chill, far away from anyone who had expectations of him. He particularly wanted to escape media attention.

The thing he hated most about his life as a *celebrity sportsman*—he loathed that label—was media intrusion into his private life. Ever since he'd been thrust into the public eye the media had published exaggerated and erroneous versions of events in his private life. A lunch date with a colleague blown up into infidelity. Such fake news had led to a rift with his former girlfriend and, even worse, the inciting incident that had led to his disastrous accident.

His return to Sydney had been purposely under the radar. He'd agreed to be best man to Alan in a low-key, private wedding. Now it seemed Alan had wanted his wedding out of the public eye for his own underhand reasons. Surprisingly to Max, the groom had not traded on the best man's celebrity. It wasn't paparazzi that had taken all those photos. It was the wedding photographer who had fully capitalised on his luck in being in the right place at a scandalous time and sold the pictures everywhere.

As a result, Max's role in the 'runaway bride' story that had so captivated Sydney had catapulted him headfirst into a rabid feeding frenzy of press speculation. Right when he'd most needed his privacy. He shuddered at the memory of it. Especially the photos of him carrying another man's bride in his arms—accompanied by salacious headlines—that had featured on magazine covers all around the world.

Boring would do him just fine. Today, he anticipated the joys of anonymity.

He'd cycled from Frangipani Bay to the village of Jungut Batu, where the fast boat service brought people from Sanur on the mainland across the Badung Strait to Nusa Lembongan.

Max had taken the fast boat ride himself the day before. On arrival, he'd enjoyed a particularly tasty *nasi goreng* from one of the local *warungs*, small family run cafés, on the road that ran parallel to the beach. He fancied trying some other speciality from the menu for lunch, washed down with an Indonesian beer. This was the first time he'd travelled so simply, blending in with the backpackers, without agenda. Already he was enjoying the slower pace.

His talent for tennis had shown up when he was barely tall enough to handle a racket. For many years afterwards, school vacations had been devoted to training. There'd been no gap years or budget bus tours around Europe with friends his own age. Later, vacations had often been linked to promoting events managed by his corporate sponsors. And always there had been tennis. Even on a luxury vacation, he'd trained every day of the year. Training on Sundays and even Christmas Day, when his rivals didn't, had helped give him the edge.

As far as he knew, there was no tennis court on Nusa Lembongan.

Already he was starting to wind down. Felt the warmth of the sun, the sparkling of the endless aquamarine sea, even the spicy scents so different from his everyday life loosening the stranglehold concern for his after-sport career had on his thoughts. The people of this part of the world were known for their warmth and friendliness— their genuine smiles were also contributing to the gradual rebirth of his well-being.

Cycling in the tropical humidity of the day had made him hot; prickles of perspiration stung his forehead, made his T-shirt cling to his back. He decided to walk down one of the narrow alleys that led from the street to the beach to cool off, maybe even plunge into the water. His clothes would dry soon enough.

A nearby boat was offloading passengers, including backpackers and tourists from all over the world. Max paused to watch them. There was no dock. Boats were tethered to shore by mooring lines that ran up the beach. Passengers were helped off the back of the boat and had to wade through the shallow waters to dry land. As people disembarked, he heard excited exclamations in German, Dutch, French, Chinese as well as English spoken in a variety of accents. Fascinated, he gazed at the local women who got off the boat then walked away with heavy boxes of supplies balanced on the tops of their heads.

A young woman with a large backpack turned to thank the boat crew with a wide, sunny smile. Idly, he wondered where she was from, where she was going. She looked like a typical backpacker in loose, brightly patterned hippy pants pulled up to her knees in preparation for her paddle through the water, a gauzy white top and a woven straw hat jammed over wind-tangled blonde hair. As she waded through the aqua-coloured water to the sand, she turned to a fellow backpacker and laughed at something he said. Max froze. That laugh, her profile, seemed familiar.

For a moment he thought… But it couldn't be. Then she turned to face the beach and he caught sight of her face full on. *No.* Not *her.* Not here. The last woman he ever wanted to see again. He blamed her in large part for the hell his life in Sydney had become.

'Terima kasih.'

Nikki thanked the crew as she left the boat to wade the few metres onto the beach shore, cool waters lapping around her calves. She'd been to Sanur to pick up supplies from the pharmacy for her friend Maya. Mission accomplished and back on Lembongan, she turned her thoughts to work and the snorkelling trip she was guiding that afternoon, currents permitting. July with its excellent weather was one of the busiest months for tourism here, coinciding with school vacations in both northern and southern hemispheres.

The island didn't get as overrun as some of the more popular areas of the main island of Bali. But in this peak season there were both day trippers and new guests arriving all the time. Tourists from all around the world seeking a more off-the-beaten-track Bali experience came to Lembongan.

As she neared the shore, she became aware of a man's intense gaze on her. The guy standing on the beach was hot. Tall, broad-shouldered, hair bleached from the sun, a sexy scruff of beard growth. Blue shorts and a white T-shirt showcased an athletic, muscular body. But she wasn't looking for masculine company. Not now. Maybe not ever. The experience with Alan had left her too shattered to imagine ever trusting another man again. She ignored the stranger.

But his gaze didn't drop. In fact it turned into a distinct glare. Was he some discontented dive-boat customer? Some of the tourists were determined to swim with the manta rays or *mola mola* fish, no matter the time of year or conditions on the day they took a tour. They didn't understand how unpredictable the sea currents could be here and would go away to vent their anger on Internet review sites. She'd prefer them to express their

disappointment to her. How would she have forgotten a man as attractive as this?

But as she got closer she realised exactly who
the man was. *Max Conway.*

Anger and frustration rose in her so bitter she
could taste it. After six months surely Alan had
given up trying to find her? Now it seemed he'd
sicced his watchdog best man onto her.

She marched across the sand to confront him.
There was no call for niceties. 'What the hell are
you doing here?' she demanded.

His blue eyes were intense with dislike. 'I could
ask the same of you.'

She didn't owe him any explanations. 'Did Alan
send you to drag me back to Sydney? If so I—'

'No. Why would he? And why would you think
I'd jump to his command if he did?'

'He hasn't stopped hunting for me.'

Max shrugged. 'That's nothing to do with me.
I haven't seen the guy since your wedding day.'
His tone was so decisive, his gaze so direct, she
believed him.

His hand went to his nose in a reflex action he
didn't seem to know he was doing. She noticed it

was slightly crooked. The slight flaw only made him look more handsome. *So it was true.*

'I believe Alan didn't take it kindly when you returned my engagement ring to him.' She felt bad about what had happened. All her fault for dragging the unwilling best man into her drama. Not that she regretted it for a moment. She still shuddered at the thought of how lucky she'd been to escape marriage to Alan.

'You heard right,' said Max. 'His response was to try to knock me out.'

She cringed. The photos of the best man and the groom brawling had been all over the press. The erroneous implication being they were fighting over her. The photographer she had hired for her wedding had cashed in big time. 'Did he break your nose when he punched you?' She found herself mirroring Max's action by touching her own perfectly intact nose.

'I've had worse injuries.' He smiled a not very pleasant smile. 'Trust me, he was hurting more than I was when I punched him back.'

Secretly, she was glad Alan had been hurt. After all he'd done to her, his ex-wives, and others she'd since found out had been damaged by his underhand behaviour, her former fiancé deserved more than a whack on the nose.

'But you were friends,' she said.

'I wouldn't go so far as to call it friendship,' he said. 'I met him at tennis camp when we were teenagers and we became mates of a kind. He wasn't good enough to make the grade competitively. When he stopped playing tennis we pretty much lost touch. Until recently. I was back in Australia after years of living abroad. He'd returned to Sydney after living in Melbourne for a long time. I was surprised when he asked me to be his best man, but he said his friends were in Melbourne.'

'By marriage number three—thwarted marriage number three, I mean—he might have run out of best-man options.' Nikki couldn't help the cynical edge to her voice.

He frowned. 'Perhaps.'

'I didn't mean that as an insult,' she said hastily. 'He was lucky to have you.'

He shrugged. 'I was the sucker who said yes.'

'So you weren't pond scum after all. Not that

I ever really thought you were.' It was a small white lie. She'd thought him pond scum by association. But when he'd picked her up and run with her in his arms, Max had redeemed himself in her eyes. There was still his media reputation as a love cheat but that had nothing to do with her.

'No. But he proved to be particularly unpleasant.' Should she offer to pay for plastic surgery on his nose? Perhaps not. He might be insulted. Besides, she hadn't been the one to swing that punch.

She looked up at him. 'I'm sorry if—'

He caught her arm. 'Can we move somewhere more private? I don't want an audience.'

She followed him to a quieter part of the beach, taking care not to trip over the mooring ropes that snaked along the sand. Max stopped under the shade of a spiky-leaved Pandanus tree. She slung off her backpack and placed it by her feet. A backpack was best for carrying shopping to keep her hands free when hopping on and off boats. 'I'm sorry for being confrontational,' she said. 'I associated you with Alan. Even though you were so kind about helping me.'

He nodded in acknowledgment of her apology. *He looked so good with that beard.* 'So why are you here if not to track me down for Alan?'

'Why does anyone come to tropical islands?' he said. 'But I don't want people to know I'm here on vacation. I'd appreciate it if you kept it quiet.'

'How long are you here for?' she asked. Most people only stayed a few days. There wasn't a lot to do if you weren't into surfing or snorkelling.

'Two weeks.'

Nikki didn't know whether to be concerned by his reply or not. Only her family and very closest friends knew where she'd fled to six months ago. She'd prefer to keep it that way.

He indicated her backpack. 'What about you? Are you here just for the day?' He didn't have to say *I hope so.* She could see it on his face, hear it in the tone of his voice.

'I live here.' There was no way she could conceal it.

'What?' She could take his alarm as an insult. But their last meeting hadn't exactly led to sunshine and moonbeams for him. The media had been ruthless in their pursuit of him after the

scandal of the wedding. Determined to drum up a romance, at the very least an affair, between the runaway bride and the best man. She'd run all the way up here. He'd been left in Sydney to bear the brunt of the intrusive attention.

'Do you remember I said I had a plan?'

He nodded.

'Well, I didn't. I escaped up here the day after the wedding to stay with my Indonesian friend while I thought about what to do. She was a boarder at the girls' school I went to in Sydney. We've been great friends ever since. She'd come to Sydney for the wedding, one of my bridesmaids, and I went home with her. I knew she'd keep my whereabouts secret. What I didn't know was that she was pregnant and suffering severe morning sickness that went on and on. She and her husband run a hotel here. I stayed to help her. And I'm still here.'

He shrugged. 'The island is small. Just four kilometres long, I believe. But large enough so we can stay out of each other's way,' he said.

'True,' she said. 'I promise to keep your whereabouts secret if you do the same for me.'

'Done,' he said. His shoulders visibly relaxed. She hadn't realised how tense their chance meeting had made him. If it weren't for what she had dragged him into six months ago she might feel hurt by his aversion to her.

'Where are you staying?' she asked. 'So I'll know which resort to steer clear of.'

'The Big Blue Bungalows in Frangipani Bay,' he said.

Nikki's mouth went suddenly dry and her heart sank somewhere below sand level. She couldn't look at him. 'It…er…might be difficult for you to avoid me. That's the hotel run by my friend Maya and her husband, Kadek. Not only do I work there, I live there.'

CHAPTER THREE

EVER SINCE HE'D helped Nikki flee her wedding, Max had been haunted by dreams of the lovely runaway bride. Dreams, not nightmares.

The real-life nightmares had been played out in his waking hours with the photos of the best man and the runaway bride splashed all over the media, rabid with speculation about a relationship between them. *'Cheater Best Man'* was one of the most innocuous. His past dating history had also been dragged out and picked over—again and again. Would they ever leave him alone?

He was, in his own way, famous. The media had become interested in him when he was still a teenager and had snatched the glory of winning the Australian Open from a much older international player. Then he'd dated a rising female tennis star until their conflicting commitments and ambitions had ended it.

Though apparently, it wasn't a juicy enough story that he and Ellen didn't make it because of their careers clashing. In London, a reporter had used an intrusive lens to shoot him and a female friend having a quiet lunch together and blown it up into a 'Love Cheat' scandal. The resulting headlines had made it impossible for him and Ellen to retain any kind of friendship. She'd been convinced he'd cheated on her while they were still together. If he ever played against her in a doubles game it was always a 'grudge match', according to the press. His love life—or lack of it—was of continuing interest.

What he hadn't realised was that Nikki had a public profile too, as daughter of a wealthy property developer and in her own right as a successful entrepreneur. That had ramped the interest in them as an illicit 'couple' up to a higher level. Those few weeks after the wedding when they were hot news had been nightmarish.

His ongoing dreams of Nikki might not be nightmares but they were unsettling.

The dream always started at the same moment. He was back at the wedding rehearsal in the church on the Thursday night before her wedding. As best man, he was standing next to Alan near the altar. Nikki walked down the aisle, slowly and gracefully, just as she had that night. She was wearing the same short, sleeveless blue dress and silver sandals. Her hair was tied back off her face in a ponytail. She carried a bunch of fake flowers so she could practise handing it to her sister, the chief bridesmaid. All just as it had been.

What differed in the dream was that Nikki veered away towards *him* not Alan. Her smile, the loving anticipation in her eyes, was for him. *He* was the groom. As she neared him he held out both hands to her and drew her close with a possessive murmur. She looked up to him and raised her face for his kiss. He dipped his head to claim her mouth—

And that was when he always woke up. Confused. Yearning. Disconsolate. Until he shook himself into consciousness and a return to common sense.

The dream was all kinds of crazy. For one thing, he had no interest in getting married. Not now when his injury had turned his life upside down. Not until his life was sorted. And not until he could be sure his marriage was for keeps. He'd seen the stresses the life of an elite sportsperson could place on a relationship. He wanted the for ever kind of happy marriage his parents had. That meant stability and certainty. Right now all his energies were single-mindedly focussed on his new post-tennis direction.

Besides, he wasn't interested in Nikki Lucas in that way. He *couldn't* be. She was attractive, yes. Not just in her looks but also her warm, engaging personality. If they'd met in other circumstances perhaps he would want to pursue that attraction. But she'd impulsively stood up her groom and left him standing at the altar. That showed a certain messiness of thought that alarmed him. Max had abandoned all the rules that had governed his life to aid and abet the runaway bride. And paid the price with his name all over the scandal sheets. *They'd both paid the price.* The only way he could deal with the adverse press was the knowledge that he had nothing to hide. He could truthfully plead he was innocent of any romantic intent towards Nikki. No affair. No ongoing relationship. *Just those cursed dreams.*

And yet here she was. Not the Nikki of his memory or his imagination. But just as lovely. Just as appealing. *Just as off-limits.* With the uncertain future that lay ahead of him, he needed to stay scandal free with no appearances in the press for the wrong reasons. His behaviour that day had been quite out of character for him. To get where he had in the ultra-competitive world of international tennis, he'd had to stay focussed. He planned. He strategised. He drove himself with iron self-discipline. He did not let his emotions get the better of him.

Now Nikki looked up at him, not with the loving gaze of his dream but eyes again narrowed with suspicion. 'How did I not know you were staying at Big Blue?' she asked. 'I help out at the check-in desk. I didn't see your name.'

'I'm checked in as Maxwell James. James is my second name. It's a privacy thing.'

Her feet were firmly planted in the sand. She

looked as combative as someone could in billowing hippy pants with the light breeze blowing her hair around her face. He noticed she didn't wear any make-up. She didn't need it. 'Why the Big Blue? Why Lembongan island? Isn't it a remarkable coincidence that you should end up here?'

'That's all it is. A coincidence. I'd never heard of the island until recently. And my travel agent booked me into the hotel. It ticked all the boxes for what I wanted.'

Her brows drew together. 'You really didn't know I was staying there?'

'Absolutely not. I would have steered clear if I'd had any idea.'

Hurt flashed across her face at his words. Max mentally slammed his hand against his forehead. 'Please don't take offence. I didn't mean to be rude. But you must realise that after our time in the headlines, I wouldn't want to see you again. To risk all the media speculation starting up afresh. That was hell.'

She took a moment to reply. 'It must have been awful for you. Being up here, I escaped the worst of it. Though my unavailability for comment sent

them into a frenzy. I stopped reading after someone claimed to have sighted me with you hiding
in a…in a love nest in Fiji.' She flushed high on
her cheekbones at the words *love nest*. Max had
to force himself not to conjure up images of how
it might play out if that were actually true.

He cleared his throat. 'Yeah. I stopped reading them after a while too. Then, thankfully, the
stories dwindled away when the next big beat-
up scandal took over. I don't want to give them
something new to gossip about.'

'Me neither,' she said fervently.

'I'll move to another hotel. Maybe you can recommend one.'

She shook her head. 'No need for that. Big Blue
is a great place to stay this end of the beach. My
friends only took it over not so long ago. They
won't want anyone cancelling a two-week book-
ing. I especially don't want that to be because of
me.'

Max didn't know how to talk about avoiding
her without sounding offensive. He remembered
how he'd felt—as if his heart were melting—at
the sight of her tears on the day of her wedding.

He didn't want to upset her, or feel any urge to comfort her. He didn't want any kind of relationship with the woman who had thrust him back into those hideous headlines. 'We'll have to steer clear of each other.'

But she didn't sound offended—in fact it seemed she wanted to avoid him as much as he wanted to avoid her. 'We can do that. For one thing I'm part of the staff, unofficially that is, and you're a guest. That means few opportunities to mingle. What room are you in? One of the *lumbung* on the beach?'

'*Lumbung?*'

'Over two levels, the traditional thatched roof, the woven bamboo ceilings, the open bathroom.'

'No. I'm in one of the two larger new villa-style bungalows further back from the beach. Number two. I have my own lap pool. I thought it would be more private than facing the beach.'

'Oh,' she said, her blush deepening. 'That… well, that could be another problem. I'm staying in the adjoining villa.'

Not just on the same island. In adjacent rooms. Nikki lying in bed just a stone wall away from him. What kind of dreams might that inspire? He swallowed a curse. 'Imagine if the media got hold of that? They'd have a field day. I *must* move to another hotel.'

She put up her hand in a halt sign. 'No. Don't do that. I'll move to the staff quarters at the back of the resort. I can have a room there. It's pretty basic but—'

'I can't allow you to do that.'

She scowled. Which made her look cute rather than fierce. 'It's not a matter of you *allowing* me to do anything. It's only for two weeks. I'm not such a "spoiled Sydney princess" that I can't deal with it.'

Her voice wobbled on the words. So she'd read that offensive story too. It had been immensely unflattering about both of them. He'd felt outraged on her behalf. Had thought about contacting her to offer his commiserations. Had decided against it. He could not be linked to her again. Besides, no one had known where she was. *Now he did.*

'And after the two weeks? What then for you?' he asked.

'Back into my own room, I guess,' she said.

'I mean, what are you doing up here?'

'Helping my friend Maya. Making plans. You know I sold my business?'

'I saw that,' he said.

The night of the rehearsal, when he'd first met Nikki, he had looked her up and read about her success story. How her sister had a very sensitive skin and couldn't use any of the commercial products. How Nikki had developed a range of products that worked for her sister. How she hadn't sought conventional distribution but got in early with her online store, stocking first her own products then other brands. Word of mouth and canny marketing had made it a very profitable hit. Just days after the wedding debacle he'd been surprised to see she'd sold out to one of the huge international cosmetic conglomerates under the headline *'Runaway Bride Cashes In'*.

'Congratulations,' he said. 'Did you sell because of what happened with Alan?'

She shook her head. 'The sale was put in motion before the wedding I thought offloading my very demanding business would give me more time to devote to…' Her voice hitched. 'To family life.'

'I'm sorry,' he said, not sure what else he could say.

She shrugged. 'As it turned out the timing was right—after all I needed a sabbatical from work, some time to put myself together again. Everything had fallen apart. I… I wasn't coping very well with the aftermath.'

'Understandably,' he said carefully.

She raised her eyes to his. 'You know, I really thought I loved Alan. And that he loved me. I'm nearly thirty. I wanted to get married and start a family. It was devastating to find out the truth about him. How horribly he'd lied. That he wasn't at all the person I'd thought he was. I didn't run away from the wedding on a whim, you know.' She scuffed the sand with the toe of her sandals, averting her gaze.

'I know you didn't,' he said. She'd been too desperate for it to have been whim. When the media speculation had been at its fieriest, he had asked himself whether, if he had the time again, he would have aligned himself with Team

Groom and refused to help her. He hadn't had to think long.

'Almost to the time I got to the church I thought I'd go through with it,' she said. 'That he'd change. That I'd be the one to make him change where other women had failed. Deep down I knew that wouldn't happen. My father came good when he went into the church to tell Alan and the guests. But in the car he wouldn't hear of helping me bolt. My behaviour would have reflected badly on him. Then I saw you and—'

'And the rest is history,' he said drily. 'I don't regret helping you. I'd do it all again.'

She looked up, her eyes widened in surprise. 'Despite the aftermath?'

'Yes,' he said.

There were two defining moments that had made him certain he'd done the right thing that day. The first was when she'd kissed him. A polite kiss of thanks. And yet for these few seconds her soft lips had been pressed against his cheek and he'd breathed in her scent he'd felt something he hadn't felt in a long time. An awareness. A stirring of excitement, more thrilling perhaps because it was forbidden. *Out of bounds.* He couldn't share that moment and the feelings it had aroused in him with her. But the second moment he could.

'When Alan went for me, there was a moment when his eyes went dead,' he said. 'All the charm and bonhomie gone, unable to mask a ruthless violence that I suspect was habitual. I was very glad I'd helped you escape marriage to the man.'

Nikki gasped and her hand went to her heart. 'You recognised that? His first ex-wife hinted at abuse on that first phone call. Then confirmed it afterwards when I sent her flowers in gratitude for the warning.'

He pushed away the unimaginable dreadful thought of Nikki suffering at the hands of her ex. Thank heaven he had been there for her. 'You had a lucky escape.'

'Yes,' she said. 'Thanks to the people who helped me.'

Max couldn't help but wonder what kind of woman would be so generous as to send flowers to the woman who had warned her off her ex-husband? She was something, Nikki Lucas.

'Why didn't I recognise him for what he was?' she said. 'How could I have been so blind?'

'If it's any consolation I was taken in by him too. Why else would I agree to be best man to a guy I hardly knew? He was persuasive. Played on a long-ago friendship. The fact I was back in Sydney after a lengthy absence and looking to establish a new circle of people.'

'Did you know I agreed to marry him after only a few months? He knew exactly how to play me,' she said with a bitter twist to her mouth. 'Made me believe that everything I wanted from life, he wanted too.'

What did Nikki want? Max realised how very little he actually knew about her. And how tempting it would be to find out more.

Nikki had not intended to confide in Max about The Abominable Alan, the nickname Maya had given her former fiancé. But it was a relief to discover that his best man had been fooled by him as well. Alan had probably had an ulterior motive in his dealings with Max, as he had with her. Max was a very wealthy man. A multimillionaire. That fact had come up again and again in the media stories about him. She wondered if Alan had approached him to invest in some dodgy enterprise.

She didn't dare ask. Max had given her the impression of being contained—a private person, in spite of his public persona as a love cheat. There were tennis players who threw tantrums, were known for bad behaviour. Not Max. He was renowned for being courteous and well-mannered on the court, the smiling assassin with his killer serve. That first night at the rehearsal, once she'd got over the shock that her groom's best man was a tennis superstar, she'd found him surprisingly reserved. She'd done her best to make him feel comfortable in a room full of people who were strangers to him. Not that it had been a hardship. Not only was Max heart-stoppingly handsome in that strong, athletic way, he'd also made her laugh with his wry comments about wedding procedure. She'd liked him. A lot.

It was ironic, she thought now, that her groom had turned out to be a stranger to her while the unknown best man had done her a favour. But even one moment of her brainpower directed towards Alan was a moment too many. Seeing Max here had brought back feelings that she'd believed six months away from her old life had insulated her against. The discovery of Alan's perfidy, the shattering of her happy-ever-after illusion had left her broken. Her time on the island had helped the healing process. She didn't want the plaster ripped off old wounds. Or any controversy about her and Max stirred up again. They each had much to gain by staying out of each other's way.

'You know we really shouldn't be standing here chit-chatting,' she said. 'I doubt anyone on this beach would recognise me. But you could be a different matter. I know your hair is longer and you're growing a beard—which by the way looks really good and suits you—but you're famous in a way I'm not. It would only take one fan to spot you and—'

'Disaster,' he said, taking a step back from her.

'May I suggest you wear a hat as a kind of disguise?' she said. 'You'll need to wear one anyway for the heat. The weather gets really steamy here.'

'It gets so hot on the uncovered courts at the

Australian Open that players have hallucinated and collapsed during a game,' he said.

'But not you?' she said with a challenging tilt of her head.

'Not me,' he said. A smile tugged at the corners of his mouth.

'You laugh at the heat?'

In response she had the full impact of the slow, lazy grin he was famed for. Her heart beat a little tattoo of awareness. *He* was hot.

'I wouldn't say that. But I grew up in the central west of New South Wales where the summers are blazing. When I wasn't playing tennis I was helping my dad on the family farm.'

She'd like to ask him about that too. *'Boy from the bush made good'* was a popular description of him. She would have to content herself with looking him up on the Internet rather than engaging in the kind of first-date conversation she could never have with him.

'It's a different kind of heat here. It took me a while to get acclimatised.' Though the temperature seemed to rise just standing near him.

'I'll take your advice and buy a hat,' he said.

She bit her tongue to stop herself from offering to help him choose a style that suited him. *Not a good idea.*

Instead she gave impersonal advice. 'There are a few shops selling hats up on the main street. Well, it's the only street, really.'

'I saw a place that seemed to sell everything including hats near the *warung* where I plan to have lunch.'

'You're having lunch here? I was going to have lunch in the village as well. I like to have a change from eating in Frangipani Bay.'

They fell suddenly, awkwardly silent. Nikki looked up into his blue, blue eyes. She was aware of the gentle swishing of the water on the sand. People from the boats calling to each other in Indonesian. Laughter that would soon turn to squeals from the tourists decked out in orange life jackets climbing aboard the banana float that would be towed out to sea at speed by a small boat.

The words hung unspoken between them. *Why not have lunch together?*

When she finally spoke she knew her words

were tumbling over each other too fast. 'Obviously that plan is out the window. I'll go straight back to Big Blue and grab a bite there. But I have a favourite café here. Excellent food. You must try it. I'll tell you the name.'

He frowned. 'Why should you miss your lunch? You go to your café. If my *warung* is too close, I'll find another one. I'm sure it's not the only one serving *nasi goreng*.'

Again the nervous giggle. *What was wrong with her?* 'It most certainly wouldn't be the only one. *Nasi goreng* and *mie goreng* are probably the most commonly served meals on the island.'

'What's the difference?' he asked.

'*Nasi goreng* is a spicy fried rice served with vegetables and maybe prawns or chicken and usually an egg. But then you know that as you've already tried it. *Mie goreng* is fried noodles made in a similar way. I actually prefer it.'

'Do you speak Indonesian?'

'A little. Quite a lot, actually. Maya taught me when we were at school. I'm much better at it than I was when I first arrived.' *Well, that was stating the obvious*. 'There are differences in

Balinese and Lembongan, of course. You won't need to worry. Everyone dealing with visitors speaks English. They learn it in school.'

If Max thought she was gabbling he didn't show it. Again that slow, lazy smile. 'That's useful to know. I wish—'

'You wish what?'

Time seemed to stop as he looked down into her face. 'You could be my guide to all things Lembongan,' he said slowly.

A dangerous thrill of anticipation shot through her. She would like that very much. 'But that can't be,' she said, stamping down firmly on that feeling.

'I know,' he said, regret underscoring his words.

'We both know we can't spend time together. Not if we don't want to risk ending up sharing headlines again. I don't think I could deal with a new onslaught of that kind of attention.'

'If we had met under different circumstances, if we were different people, perhaps—' She felt her heartbeat trip up a gear. *What was he saying?*

'Perhaps?'

'It would be a different story,' he said abruptly.

Nikki wasn't sure that was what he had intended to end his *perhaps* with but there was little point in pursuing it. It was enough to know that the spark of interest wasn't completely one-sided. Not that she could do anything about it.

'So how should we handle this, Maxwell James? Pretend we don't know each other?'

'That could work,' he said.

'We'll make it work,' she said. 'We'll have to take Maya and Kadek into our confidence. She was there on the church steps. She saw it all.'

His eyes narrowed. 'Can you trust her?'

'Absolutely without question,' she said. She took a deep breath, took a step back from him. 'We need to start as we mean to continue. You go your way and I go mine. Strangers who happened to chat with each other on the beach about the difference between fried rice and fried noodles.'

'Yes,' he said. Was that regret shadowing his eyes? Or just the reflection of her own feelings?

'How did you get here to the village?' she asked.

'I rode one of the hotel's mountain bikes.'

'That was brave of you. The roads in some

places are more potholes than surface and there doesn't seem to be much in the way of road rules.'

'I noticed,' he said in the understated way she was beginning to appreciate. 'You?'

'The hotel truck will come to pick me up when I'm ready.'

'The troop carrier?'

She smiled. 'That's one way of describing the taxis here.'

Transport on the island comprised mainly open-backed trucks where the passengers sat facing each other on parallel benches in the back. No seat belts. No safety rules like back home. It had taken some getting used to. But the drivers were considerate and courteous. And now Nikki never gave the fact she could be risking her life every time she climbed on board a second thought. That was how you lived here and there was a certain freedom to it that she liked. There were different risks and perils back in Sydney.

She reached down to pick up her backpack from where it rested on the sand. Max leaned down at the same time. 'Let me carry that for you.' Their hands brushed just for a moment as he reached for the strap but long enough for that same electric feeling that had tingled through her when he'd carried her over the threshold. She snatched her backpack back to her.

'That's very chivalrous of you. Again. But to see you carrying my bag might kind of give the game away, mightn't it?'

'I get that,' he said. 'But it goes against the grain to let you lift that heavy pack.'

'Must be your rural upbringing,' she said. It was part of the Max Conway mythology that he'd started playing tennis on a rundown community court in a tiny town in the central west of New South Wales.

'There's that. But I grew up seeing my father treat my mother well. He would have done that wherever we lived.'

'How refreshing,' she said, unable to suppress the note of bitterness from her voice. She seemed to have spent a good deal of her twenty-nine years around men for whom treating women well was not a priority. Like her father—now divorced from wife number three. Like her cheating high-school boyfriend with whom she'd wasted way too many years in a roller coaster of a relation-ship. And then there was Abominable Alan.

'It's not always appreciated,' he said. Nikki re-membered that as part of the 'best man betrayal' frenzy, one of the big women's magazines had run an interview with Max's hometown girlfriend who had nursed a grudge against him. Just an-other in a line of 'love cheat' stories about him.

'Trust me, I would appreciate it,' she said with rather too much fervour. 'But I've been looking after myself for a long time and am quite okay about carrying my own backpack.'

She picked up the bag and heaved it onto her back. It would have been crass to shrug off his help with getting the straps in place across her back. Even if she did have to grit her teeth against the pleasurable warmth of his touch through the fine cotton fabric of her top.

'Feel okay?' he asked as he adjusted the strap.

'Fine,' she said as nonchalantly as she could manage with the sensation of his fingers so close to her skin. *It wasn't the balance of the backpack that felt fine but his touch.* 'It's not very heavy, anyway.'

She straightened her shoulders. 'Now you need to go your way and I need to go mine. You head off up the alley through those two shops. It will take you onto the street. The café I like is to the right, so you turn to the left. About six shops down there's a great little *warung* serving Balinese food.'

'Hey, that's the place I was heading for with the great *nasi goreng.* Seems you know what pleases me.'

'Just a lucky guess,' she said, flustered by his tone, not wanting to meet his gaze.

'If I see you on the street, I ignore you, right?' he said. 'No hard feelings?'

'No hard feelings,' she said. 'I'll do the same.'

She watched him as he strode away. His back view was as impressive as his front—broad shoulders tapering to a tight butt, lean muscular legs. He was a spectacular athlete on court, leaping and twisting high in the air to connect with the ball in an incredible reach. Not that she'd ever taken much notice before their encounter at her wedding. But in her down time here on the island, she'd discovered there were many online videos of Max Conway's greatest sporting achievements to enjoy.

As he headed towards the street, she realised she wasn't the only one admiring his good looks and athletic grace. A group of attractive girls watched him too, through narrowed, speculative eyes. For a heart-stopping moment Nikki thought they recognised him. But no. They just thought he was hot.

So, heaven help her, did she.

CHAPTER FOUR

LATER THAT AFTERNOON, Max sat out by the lap pool under the shade of a frangipani tree in the small, private courtyard outside his room. He was trying to concentrate on a proposal from his agent for a new role—something very different that had potential to be either an exciting new direction or a monumental sell-out. But the words on the screen blurred before his eyes.

There was no reason he should feel so distracted. This place was a private paradise. His one-bedroom suite was spacious and comfortable, traditional with its thatched peaked roof and woven bamboo ceiling, modern in its stylishly appointed open-air shower and air-conditioning.

The courtyard was surrounded by high stone walls and planted with a profusion of lush, tropical plants. The pool was long enough to swim laps, the water cool and sparkling. It was quiet, with just the occasional cooing of doves and echoes of distant laughter coming from somewhere else in the resort to break the silence. The place had everything he'd wanted for his vacation. Seclusion. Privacy. Time alone with his thoughts.

Trouble was his thoughts were no longer his own. *Nikki Lucas.* Since their encounter earlier in the day she had been flitting in and out of his mind, getting in the way of everything else, tripping up his concentration.

As if the recurring dream weren't bad enough, now he was haunted by the image of her on the beach, laughing up at him, the turquoise sea behind her, green glints in her warm brown eyes, her gauzy shirt clinging to her curves. She had agreed so readily to stay out of his way. As wary, it seemed, as he was about adverse publicity. It was refreshing that she wasn't grasping after him.

He was used to women who, when it came to him, had an agenda. He was wealthy. Wealthier even, thanks to canny investments, than many people suspected. Reasonably good-looking.

And, until the elbow incident, at the top of his game. That brought with it a lot of female attention. Not all of it the right type. At first he'd been dazzled by the attention—what red-blooded young man wouldn't be? But he'd soon learned he wasn't a bed-hopping kind of guy. He wanted more, a real relationship, a partnership, but his dedication to his career made that something for the future. Along the way, he'd been burned by women with no interest in him as himself, as just Max, but instead only as a celebrity sports star and what they could get from him.

Even his high-school girlfriend, Lisa, had proved herself to be not immune to the lure of his bank account. From the get-go he'd made it clear he could not commit to her. That his career, with its arduous training schedules and constant travel, came first and would for a long time. He'd broken up with her when he'd moved away for good.

But he'd held happy memories of her and in a moment of nostalgia had hooked up with her on a whirlwind visit to his parents. Only later to be hit by news she'd had a baby and a demand for child support. If it had been true, he would have totally stepped up to his responsibilities. But a DNA test had proved he was not the father. How the episode had leaked to the press he had no idea. But the speculation had not been pleasant. Though how they'd made *him* out to be the 'love cheat' in that case had been beyond him.

Perhaps Lisa's resentment of him had been behind her recent hostile interview where she'd claimed he was selfish, without scruples, and exactly the kind of man who would run away with his friend's bride just because he could. He shuddered at the memory of it—her words, untrue though they were, had hurt. No wonder he was wary, didn't easily place his trust in women. No wonder he hated the intrusion of the media.

But Nikki seemed different. After all, she'd already got what she'd wanted from him—help to escape from her wedding. He had done so and moved on. She needn't have any further role in his life. Avoiding her should be easy.

He forced his attention back to the screen. All of his adult years had been devoted to tennis—and a good deal of his young years as well. His tennis career had meant a tight schedule where every minute of every twenty-four hours was arranged and accounted for. Others had laughed to discover that he practised even on Christmas Day—but he'd felt the joke was on the people who didn't train at his level of intensity. It gave him the edge.

But deciding on a new direction that would satisfy his need to excel was not proving to be straightforward. It wasn't that he needed the money. He need never work again if he didn't want to. But he wanted a purpose, something to drive him forward, a focus. Sitting still had never been his thing. By the time he'd spent two weeks here he was determined to have made a final decision.

Just minutes later, he was surprised by the chiming of the wind chimes hanging by the gate that acted as a doorbell. He hadn't ordered room service. And it was too early for the bed to be turned down.

He opened the ornately carved wooden doors at the entrance to the courtyard. Nikki stood at the threshold. She was carrying a circular wooden tray of snack-sized foods wrapped in banana leaves and an array of sliced fruit, which she held out in front of her like an offering. Max was too surprised to do anything but stare.

She was dressed in the hotel staff uniform of a batik patterned sarong in shades of blue and a hip-length white lacy blouse, finished with a wide blue sash around her trim waist. Her hair was pulled tightly back from her face in a small bun into which was tucked a spray of delicate white flowers. The effect was both charming and quietly alluring. While modest, the outfit discreetly outlined her shape making no secret of the swell of her breasts, the curve of her hips. *She was beautiful.*

But what was she doing there? 'Nikki! I thought we'd agreed not to—'

She gave a quick, furtive glance over her shoulder. From where he stood it didn't seem that anyone was observing them. 'May I come in?' She sidled through the gate and pushed it shut behind her with her hip. 'Indonesian afternoon tea,' she explained. 'Delivering it made a good excuse for me to visit your room.'

Bemused, he took the tray from her, inhaled the delicious spicy aromas that wafted upwards. The food was enticing, it had been a while since lunch, but his thoughts were firmly on Nikki. He placed the tray on the nearby outdoor table.

'I'm sorry but it turns out I can't move into the staff quarters,' she said. 'Maya has assigned the room to a new housekeeper. The rest of the resort is completely booked out. That means—'

'You're still next door.' Why was there elation mingled with his dismay?

'I'm afraid so. My first thought was I could move out for the duration of your stay, perhaps to the mainland. But Maya begged me not to. It's their busiest time. The baby is very young. She needs me.'

'Then there's no choice but for me to move out to the mainland. That would solve any proximity problem.' *He would never see her again.*

Her eyes widened in alarm. 'Please don't do that. Sooner or later the news will get out that you booked in here. Hopefully long after there could be any connection to me. But for a celebrity like you to cancel his stay would be bad publicity for

Big Blue. Kadek's family is in the hotel business. This place was run down and badly managed when they bought it. Kadek is a second son. It's his chance to prove himself by making a success of it. His and Maya's.'

Max gave himself time to think. 'Is it such a big deal to be in next-door villas? After all, there are no connecting doors.'

Her eyes brightened. 'Keep to our own side of those high stone walls and there shouldn't be a problem.'

He knew she was as worried about them being seen together as he was. Yet she was prepared to risk it for her friend. Her loyalty to Maya was appealing. Besides, what she said made sense. He looked around him. The high walls, the frangipani trees, the screen of large-leaved foliage acted like barricades against the outside world. Then he looked back to her. 'It's so secluded and private, right now no one would know we were here alone together.'

As if every throbbing cell in her body weren't aware of that. Of her proximity to one of the hottest ever sports stars in the world. Nikki knew the media interest in the scandalous runaway bride and the best man wasn't because of her but because of public fascination with *him*.

She could quite see why. Max was wearing only a pair of black swim shorts. He must recently have been in the pool. His hair was slicked dark and drops of water glistened on his broad shoulders, the super defined muscles of his chest and arms, his flat belly. Nikki had to force her gaze away. It was a real effort to maintain a conversation with him. She'd had to hand him the afternoon tea tray as she'd feared she might drop it because of hands that were suddenly shaky. Now she concentrated on three creamy frangipani blossoms that were floating on the surface of the pool. *Eyes off the best man.*

'You're right.' She forced her voice to sound normal. 'If we're careful, there's no need for either of us to move out of our accommodation.'

'That's done, then. You stay on your side of the wall and I'll stay on mine. But while you're here…' His eyes strayed to the tray of snacks on the table. 'That's like no afternoon tea I've ever seen. I suspect those intriguing parcels would go very well with a cold beer. Join me?'

Nikki glanced down at her watch. She was scheduled to help out on the desk but not just yet. 'Do you think it's wise for me to stay?'

He shrugged those magnificent broad, very naked shoulders. 'Probably not. But you're here, it's private and you're dressed as staff. I think we'd be safe.'

She pushed aside the promptings of her better judgement. 'I'll pass on the beer as I'm due soon at the reception desk. But a cold mineral water would be welcome.'

He headed inside the sliding glass door to the bar fridge. Nikki felt light-headed at the sight of him. She flushed and had to hold onto the back of a chair to steady herself. Could a man have a better rear view? At the beach, she'd thought he'd looked good in his shorts and T-shirt. But with those impressive muscles flexing under sun-tanned skin and damp swim shorts moulding the best butt she'd ever seen, her appreciation level shot off the scale.

Sadly, when he returned with the bottle of

water and a glass, he'd put on a T-shirt. Covering up that chest was a crime. Inwardly, she sighed. Perhaps it was for the best. She couldn't allow herself to fancy Max Conway. She couldn't trust herself to fancy any man. Not after the monumental error of judgement she'd made with Alan. Come to think of it, she'd never been a good judge of men. Seeing in them what she wanted to see, not the reality that they were after nostrings fun or access to her money. Perhaps both. Leaving her with her heart broken and wondering where she'd gone wrong. Feeling like a fool.

'You look flushed,' he said. *If only he knew!*

'Er, yes. It is very hot today.'

'Sit down in the shade and have a cool drink,' he said.

Nikki took the cane chair he offered, one of four set around an outdoor table under the shade of a sweetly scented frangipani tree. She had the exact same furniture in her villa. But no outrageously handsome man solicitously pouring her a drink. 'Thank you,' she said. 'Just what I needed.'

He was just what she needed.

She pushed the errant thought from her mind.

For six months she had been without a man's company. Wasn't sure she ever wanted to link her life with a man again. *Needs*, though. That was a different matter. The presence of Max Conway, all six feet two of him, sitting just knee-nudging distance apart was reminding her that her body had needs even if her heart had been put on hold.

She edged her chair a less distracting distance away from him, making the excuse of moving it further into the shade.

Max pushed the wooden tray closer to her. 'What am I looking at here? Samosa? Spring rolls?'

'Spring rolls are called *lumpia* here and those fried pastries are like Indian samosas. There's also *ayam sisit*, which is a shredded chicken dish, and a selection of spicy savoury fritters. For something sweet there's *dadar gulung*, a yummy coconut pancake, fried banana, then fresh pineapple and papaya.'

'You choose first,' he said. 'Be quick. I could probably demolish the whole tray in two minutes.'

She laughed. 'I guess a sportsman would eat a lot.'

Again she was treated to that big, lazy smile. 'I've had to watch every bite I eat for so long. Followed strict dietary guidelines for optimum performance. Had a nutritionist rapping me on the knuckles if I strayed. Now I'm eating what I want. I have a big appetite and love good food.'

Another of those disconcerting shivers of awareness travelled down her spine. Nikki refused to speculate about his other appetites. She really shouldn't be here alone with him. Thank heaven he'd put on that T-shirt, though it really didn't do much to disguise the strength and power of his awesome body.

She wasn't very hungry so she nibbled on a spicy vegetable samosa then a piece of papaya with a squeeze of lime juice. As Max reached out for his third snack, she noticed a small scar on his elbow, white against his tan. 'How is your elbow now? Is it fully healed?'

He stopped with a *lumpia* halfway to his mouth, put it back down on its banana-leaf wrapping. All trace of humour fled from his face and the air seemed to chill around him. 'Why do you ask?' he said, eyes narrowed.

Had she said the wrong thing? Didn't the whole world know he had injured his elbow in a spectacular manner? 'I was thinking—not that I think much about you, of course I don't—that this is summer in the Northern Hemisphere and the tennis season and you—'

'Should be competing?' His expression was bleak and Nikki wished she'd never raised the subject.

'Well, yes,' she said. 'I'm sorry I brought it up.'

'Don't be sorry. It's a valid question. One that more people than you have been asking. I can't avoid answering it any longer.' He sighed, a great heaving of manly shoulders that made her want to reach out and comfort him. But even a reassuring hand on his arm wouldn't be appropriate. Not when they couldn't even be friends because of the scandal that linked them—the fear of it erupting again when she was healing from her emotional wounds. 'Fact is, the elbow is healed. But not well enough to take the stress of competitive tennis.'

'Oh,' she said, not sure what else to say. She

couldn't say she was sorry again. 'I'm sad to hear that.'

'The injury was serious. Tendons torn. Bone fractured. From the get-go, the doctors weren't optimistic that I'd ever get the strength back in it. But I refused to give into that diagnosis. I spent a year in intense rehab at a facility in California. I had orthodox treatments by the top practitioners in their field. Unorthodox treatments that seemed to have more hope than science behind them. I was willing to try anything.'

The anguish in his voice gave her no hope for optimism on his behalf. 'But nothing worked?'

'For everyday use, thankfully my arm is good. But not for elite tennis. If I can't play at the top of my form I don't want to play at all. No exhibition matches. No charity matches. There's been no announcement yet, but I'm retiring. That's another reason I'm staying out of the spotlight.'

There was a depth of sadness to his words that struck at Nikki's heart. 'I can't begin to imagine how difficult this is for you.' There was a fine line between sympathy and pity and she didn't want to cross it.

He shrugged but his voice was strained when he spoke. 'I'm not the first athlete it's happened to and I won't be the last. The constant risk of injury is something we live with. Every elite sportsperson has to move on at some time or another.'

'But you weren't ready.'

'At twenty-eight I was nearing the peak of my game.' Regret tinged with bitterness underscored his voice.

'With a serve speed of over one hundred and fifty-five miles an hour?'

'That's right,' he said.

She paused. 'I'm trying to see a silver lining here, but is it a good thing that you got out at your peak?'

'*If* that was indeed my peak. I felt I had further to go. Now I'll never know what I could have achieved.'

The depth of sadness and regret in his voice tore at her heart. She had to try and cheer him up. Without giving into the temptation to give him a hug. 'How many people come nowhere near what you achieved? In any field, not just tennis. You can be really proud of your amazing career.'

His mouth had turned down and she saw the effort he made to force it into the semblance of a smile. 'That's what my dad says. He's always been my number one cheerleader. My mum too. I've spent a lot of time with them over the last months, coming to terms with it.'

But no significant other to discuss his future with? *Not that it would matter to her.*

'So,' she said, not sure how far to go with her questions. 'What will you do?'

He shrugged those impressive shoulders. 'I've never done anything but played tennis. I started a university degree but it was impossible to continue with my sporting commitments. I never really thought beyond tennis. I'm in the same boat as many sports people who didn't plan beyond the next game.'

Only not all of them were multimillionaires. 'Someone as talented and well known as you must have options coming at you from all sides,' she said.

'There are offers on the table. That's one reason I came here. To consider them. And it's another reason I can't get caught up in any further scandal. The role I favour most is with a company with very conservative owners.'

At the pointed reminder, she wiggled uncomfortably in her chair. 'And here's potential scandal, sitting right next to you eating your papaya.'

She was relieved to see some of the tension lift from his face and the return of that engaging smile. 'If you put it that way,' he said.

'Seriously though,' she said. 'I feel for you. It wasn't easy for me to sell my business. I started it from nothing. So much slog went into it. It was my baby.' Though at the time she'd been happy to trade it for a fat cheque and the prospect of a real baby in her arms. 'I thought I might feel rudderless without it.'

'Do you?'

'Surprisingly, no. Since I've been up here I'm dreaming up new ideas.' Now with no prospect of a family anywhere in the near future—if ever— she needed a new business baby to keep her occupied.

She'd put her cosmetics business before everything, social life, dating. According to her sister, Kaylie, she had done that as much to prove herself to her father as to help Kaylie with her skin allergies.

But Nikki had never really wanted to hear that. Her relationship with her father was fraught at the best of times. Deep down she didn't know if she could ever forgive him for the death of her mother. She had died just a few days after Nikki's twenty-first birthday of a fast-acting form of breast cancer. Nikki and her sister were convinced their mum had died of a broken heart. She'd never got over the discovery of her husband's infidelity with a much younger woman on his sales team, the subsequent divorce and her father's hasty remarriage. But Nikki had no intention of discussing that aspect of her life with Max.

'Did Alan know you were planning to sell your business?' Max's face tightened and she realised there really was no love lost there. The groom had shown his true colours to the best man. Along with his fist.

'Yes. He pressed me to sell. In hindsight, I think that's the only reason he proposed—the prospect of sharing in the bounty.'

Max frowned. 'Surely you don't believe that was the only reason?'

'Looking at what he turned out to be, I can only conclude he was marrying me for my money. His anger when I ran away from him was more about loss of a potential windfall rather than of his bride.'

She knew she had failed to keep the hurt from her voice. In spite of what a jerk her former fiancé had been, in spite of her full knowledge of her lucky escape, that fact still chipped away at her self-esteem. How could she ever again trust her judgement of a man's character?

Max leaned over towards her. He frowned. 'You can't be serious. You're smart, beautiful, kind—what man wouldn't thank his lucky stars you'd want him in your life?'

His gaze drilled into hers for a moment too long. 'Uh, theoretically speaking, of course,' he said, leaning back into his chair.

'Of course,' she echoed, dropping her eyes, unable to stop her spirits from lifting. *He thought she was beautiful.* 'Thank you for those kind words.' It was amazing how soothing they were.

'True words,' he said. 'Every one of them.'

She glanced down at her watch. 'I'd love to hear more. But duty calls from the reception desk.'

But she made no move to get up from her chair, reluctant to go. This kind of chat with Max wasn't likely to happen again and she was enjoying his company. Not because he was a famous tennis star sharing his doubts and hopes for the future but because she felt relaxed in his company. *She liked him.*

But she shouldn't. *Like, love, lust.* All were off the agenda for her. She no longer trusted herself to know the difference. She wasn't ready to think about men. Not for a long time. If ever.

Max indicated the tray. 'Have some more fruit before you go. Or take that last samosa.'

'You have it,' she said. 'I really do have to go.' Not just because duty called but also because it was disconcerting to be so close to him sharing food and conversation. *Enjoying it too much.*

Max reached for the samosa. As he picked it

up, the fried pastry cracked to reveal the filling. Nikki jumped up from her chair. 'Max. Be careful. Don't—'

Too late. He bit into the pastry with gusto, then stilled, spluttered, swore, and threw the remaining half on the table. What was left of a big, mean green chilli pepper protruded from the pastry. Max's face flushed red as he pushed away from the table and stumbled up, clutching his mouth. 'Chilli. Burning. Agony.' He repeated the same swear word six times in a row.

He went to grab her bottle of mineral water. Nikki stopped him with her hand on his wrist. 'No. Water will make it worse. Milk. I'll get some.' She ran into his room to retrieve from the refrigerator the milk provided for coffee and tea. She didn't waste time pouring it in a glass but thrust the ceramic jug at him. 'Swill the milk around your mouth. It will help neutralise the burn.'

'Thanks,' he choked out as he gulped down the milk.

She handed him a piece of pineapple. 'Try this, too. The acid in the fruit helps with the heat.'

He followed instructions. She didn't try to engage him in conversation. Eventually a smile struggled through his obvious discomfort. 'I didn't know you were a nurse, Miss Scandal in Waiting.'

She was so concerned that she hadn't warned him about how hot some of the local food could be that she barely smiled her acknowledgment of his teasing comment. 'I got caught out by the heat in the chillies when I first arrived here. I know how much it burns.' She grimaced at the memory of her first encounter with those particular chillies. 'The one you just ate had seeds and the pith and they give lots of extra heat.'

Max went to wipe his mouth. 'Don't touch!' Again she stayed his hand with hers, her fingers resting on his wrist. She noticed his pulse accelerated, no doubt from effect of the chilli on his system. 'Let the milk and the acid of the pineapple do their work. The pain will ease.'

He rolled his eyes. 'I come up here for some

peace and quiet and get burned. Max Conway, unbeaten champion, felled by a chilli.'

'I saw it too late to warn you. I should have thought—'

'After all those years of never eating anything that might upset my stomach before a tournament and I bite into *that*. I didn't know they grew chillies that hot.'

'I feel so bad about it. I wish I'd taken you up on the offer to eat it instead of—'

Before she could finish her words, Max started to laugh. His blue eyes were lit with humour, his laugh was deep and rumbling and utterly infectious. After a startled pause, Nikki started to laugh too, so hard she bent over from her waist. Her laugh ended in splutters but when she looked up at him again he widened his eyes and it set them both off again.

Somehow during the laughter her hand on his arm had become her hand in his hand and she was standing close to him. Now his fingers moved to hold her hand firm. 'If you feel so bad about it, why not share the burn?' he said.

Then his lips were on hers. Briefly. Fleetingly. Her lips tingled and her heart raced at the contact. 'Do you feel it?' he murmured against her mouth. Shaken, she pulled away. Not from the slight buzz of the chilli on her lips. But from the other sensations coursing through her. Awareness. Excitement. The dizzying impact of his closeness.

'I feel it,' she said shakily, all laughter dissipated by the heat of that sizzling kiss. Heat that had not been generated by anything as straightforward as the chemical compound *capsaicinoid* that lurked in the chilli.

He wasn't laughing either. 'So did I,' he said, his voice unsteady. She wasn't talking about the chilli. Was he?

This was too much. The empathy she'd felt when he'd told her about his injury. The pleasure in his company. The flare of awareness at that fleeting touch of his mouth, not intended as a kiss, she felt sure, but as a sort of meaningless game. She found him too attractive to be playing with this kind of emotional fire. She had to stay away from him. Not just because of the need to avoid any kind of publicity and the risk of further scandal. But for the sake of preserving her own hard-won composure.

She pulled her hand away from his. 'I have to go,' she said and fled. The last thing she wanted while she healed from the deep emotional wounds caused by her encounter with a liar and a fraud was any kind of involvement with a well-publicised love cheat.

CHAPTER FIVE

MAX HADN'T BEEN anywhere near Nikki for a day. To be precise, it had been two long nights and an entire day. A few times he'd seen her in the distance. Once walking head to head in deep discussion with a beautiful young Indonesian woman he assumed was Maya. Another when she was alone and rushing along the wooden pathways that connected the various areas of the resort.

But her eyes hadn't made contact with his. Either she hadn't seen him or she'd pretended not to see him. He couldn't feel offended because it was what they had agreed. She might very well be angry with him. He had not kept to his side of the bargain with that impulsive kiss. *Feel my chilli burn.* He cringed at the thought of it. Of all the stupid moves in the book he had to pick that one. With a woman who had made it very clear she had no interest in him. Who was, anyway, out of bounds. *He had to keep it that way.*

The resort was proving more than big enough for two people intent on avoiding each other. Not so the proximity of their rooms. Despite those high stone walls, he was aware of her presence in the villa next door. The odd snatch of music. The gentle splish-splash of someone swimming in her lap pool. Did she swim in a bikini? Or nothing at all? The courtyard was secluded enough for the latter. Then there was the shower—open to the sky, and paved with smooth pebbles. In the still of the early morning, he'd heard the splash of water coming from what he thought must be her bathroom and driven himself crazy with imagining her in there as she showered, soaping her lithe body, holding her face up to the water as if for a kiss.

That he heard evidence of Nikki being in residence so close by had nothing to do with the fact he'd pushed the outdoor tables and chairs nearer to the common wall. That was just to take advantage of the shade as he worked through the despatches from his manager. Or the moonlight as he drank a solitary beer by his pool.

Then there was that darn dream.

He'd had it again last night. The same but different. This time his lips actually brushed hers before he woke, seething with the same mixed emotions the dream always aroused. It didn't take much thought to link the progression of the dream to that real-time kiss they'd shared. That impulsive ill-thought-out move had generated heat that had nothing to do with the chilli and everything to do with Nikki's sweet laughter, the scent of flowers in her hair, her slender warm body close to his. The realisation that not only did he find her very attractive—a given since the moment he'd met her on the eve of her wedding to another man—but also he found her so easy to talk to.

He wasn't a guy who easily shared confidences and yet he'd found himself opening up to her. In truth, he hadn't enjoyed a woman's company as much for a very long time. But he was also a man who did not let his life run on impulse. This time on the island was scheduled for serious career planning. Not distraction by a woman. Especially one who, if he was seen with her, could drive his name back into those hideous headlines. The kiss had been a bad idea. *It couldn't happen again.*

Because of all those very serious reasons, he found it difficult to admit to himself that it was driving him crazy not being able to see her. Even though it made utter sense not to. Just because he enjoyed her company didn't make the fact that further scandal, if he were to be linked to her, could be any less disastrous. The directorship he'd been offered was with a very conservative company. People could speculate all they liked about his role in the 'runaway bride' scandal but the truth was he had had no relationship with the bride. To appear ethical, he had to keep it that way.

As he stood beneath his own outdoor shower, he reflected that so far his time on Lembongan was working out as he'd intended. He was getting all the privacy he needed. All the quiet time to reflect. But he was on edge, restless. *Since when had private become lonely?*

After a lifetime of extreme activity he was already going a little stir crazy. He was used to his life being timetabled to the max. In years past, he'd had so little chance to relax he didn't really know how to do it. The word had never been part of his lexicon. He wasn't dealing well with 'civilian' life after the regimented life his tennis career had demanded. No wonder he was spending too much time thinking about Nikki. It might be an idea to return to a timetable allocating time for exercise, eating, time at the computer, sleeping.

As a start, he'd booked a snorkelling trip for this morning. He'd told the guy at the desk yesterday afternoon he wasn't interested in being one of a boatload of tourists. The guy had suggested he engage a small traditional fishing boat, known as a *jukung*, manned by a fisherman who knew the local tides and currents. He'd also need to hire a guide.

Max had refused a guide until it had been gently pointed out that the currents were notoriously unpredictable around the island and could be very dangerous. That local knowledge was required to find the reefs with the best coral and tropical fish. And that, for safety reasons, the hotel could never recommend that a guest snorkel alone. Reluctantly Max had agreed.

He had always enjoyed the water. He'd grown up swimming in creeks and billabongs in the country town where he grew up. The annual family vacation had involved the long trek to the coast, usually Sydney but sometimes Queensland and the Great Barrier Reef. Until the family vacation had no longer included him because he'd been playing tennis. He now realised how narrow the focus of his life had become—the process starting when he was scarcely out of his teens.

At school, he'd been encouraged to compete in the pool but tennis had already taken a hold of him and his competitive efforts had been directed there. Later, swimming had been relegated to part of his training regime. Backstroke and freestyle helped build muscular endurance and strengthened the upper body and shoulders, which powered his serve.

In recent years there hadn't been much chance to swim for pleasure. Let alone snorkel at leisure in warm, tropical waters.

He'd bought himself some fins, a mask and

snorkel in a small dive shop not far from the hotel. No need for a wetsuit in these warm waters. He ate the breakfast he'd had delivered to the room and headed down to the bay for an early start. He felt truly excited for the first time since he'd been on the island. Except for when he'd given beautiful Nikki that red-hot-chilli kiss. But that was a very different kind of excitement.

As he walked down to the bay through the hotel's lush, tropical gardens, Max marvelled at the colour of the sea glistening in every shade of aquamarine interspersed with darker blues. At nine a.m. the sun was already hot, burning down from a blue sky. He was glad he'd worn the hat Nikki had suggested he buy.

His spirits lifted even further when he saw the small traditional outrigger fishing boat, powered by an outboard motor, moored near the beach. It was painted bright yellow and red. He thought it looked like a water spider floating on the calm turquoise surface of the bay. As he made his way down the sand, the boatman waved him over with a cheerful greeting.

The guide seemed to be already in the boat,

with his back to Max, wearing a black top and leaning over to rummage under the seat in the front of the boat. The boat was small, no more than five metres long by his estimation, and Max wondered if there would be enough room for him and two other men.

But as Max neared the boat the guide turned. Not a man but Nikki, wearing a black swim shirt over a red swimsuit, pulling out a life jacket from where it had been stored under the wide slat that formed a seat. She looked ready to call a greeting but her eyes widened in alarm and she dropped the life jacket when she saw him.

'What are you doing here?' she said at the same time he spoke.

'What are you doing on my boat?' he said.

'Your boat? It's not your boat. It's booked for...' She straightened up to face him, her eyes narrowed. 'You must be James.'

'*Mister* James,' he said.

'The desk told me I was guiding for a man named James.' The drawing together of her eyebrows said *I didn't expect it to be you.*

Max was aware they had an audience of the

boatman and the people already basking in the sun on the beach. They had an agreement to act in public as though they didn't know each other. 'And you are?' he said.

She cleared her throat. Obviously not a natural-born liar or used to pretence. 'Nikki,' she choked out. 'Your snorkelling guide.'

He decided to give her an 'out'. 'Pleased to meet you, Nikki,' he said. 'But I don't need a guide. I'm a strong swimmer and I've snorkelled before.'

She shook her head. 'You have to have a guide. These beautiful waters can be deceptively dangerous to people who don't know them. Wild, spinning undercurrents can come from nowhere. You cannot go out alone.' She indicated the boatman. 'Wayan grew up around here. He knows how to read the waters, be aware of changes in weather. If he thought it wasn't safe, we wouldn't be going out today. But he stays on the boat. You need someone with you in the water.'

'And that would be you.' He tried to keep the sudden surge of pleasure at the thought out of his voice.

'Yes. But I can try and find someone else for you if you'd rather not go with me as your guide.' Now she was giving him an out.

'That won't be necessary...Nikki,' he said. 'If I'm going to have a guide I'm happy for it to be you.'

Happier than he should be considering their agreement to stay out of each other's way, considering the awkwardness he felt that the last time they'd met he'd kissed her and she'd turned and run from him.

He couldn't tell whether she was glad or annoyed that he hadn't chosen to have another guide. She nodded. 'I'm a certified dive instructor and though I'm not a local I have extensive experience of diving and snorkelling here. Between me and Wayan, you'll be in good hands.'

Max thought about that. 'I surrender myself to your hands,' he said. She flushed high on her cheekbones and glared at him. 'And Wayan's hands, of course,' he added.

'With pleasure, Mr James,' she said coolly.

Max put his waterproof bag containing his snorkelling gear and a bottle of water onto the boat, then stepped over the outrigger to climb on board. With his added weight, the boat rocked from side to side. Nikki put her hand on his arm to steady him. He didn't really need it—good balance was a skill that served a tennis player well—but he left it there because he liked it.

She took the opportunity to lean in towards him to whisper, 'How did this happen?' Today she smelled of salt and fresh air and the lemongrass shampoo provided in their bathrooms.

'I have no idea,' he replied in a hushed undertone. 'I inquired about snorkelling at the desk at Big Blue and the guy suggested hiring Wayan's boat. He also stressed the unpredictable currents and insisted he book me a guide. He didn't say who it would be and I didn't ask.'

'He wasn't to know we knew each other, or how. Only Maya and Kadek know we're acquainted.'

He didn't want to get off that boat. 'Perhaps it's not such a big deal. No one is likely to see us out at sea. And a mask and snorkel would be a good disguise.'

'We still need to be careful,' she cautioned.

'There are quite a lot of people on the beach. There will be other boats out there too, though you make a good point about the mask.'

'It's agreed we'll be careful,' he said, tugging his hat down further over his face.

Nikki pulled away from him, as far as she could in the very confined space of the narrow boat. 'So, let's enjoy our time snorkelling,' she said out loud, speaking as impersonally as if she were, indeed, a total stranger to him. 'I'll need to get you a larger life jacket.' She reached back under the seat and handed him an orange life jacket. Then strapped herself into a smaller one. She spoke a few words to Wayan in Indonesian and within minutes the boat headed out of Frangipani Bay.

Max sat next to her on the wooden bench that spanned the boat. It was just wide enough so they could sit without touching, even with their torsos bulked up by the life jackets. She didn't talk, just looked straight ahead, calm, unconcerned. But she betrayed herself by the way she nervously twisted the strap of her life jacket.

Max looked straight ahead too. 'I…uh…must

apologise about the incident with the chilli.' He couldn't bring himself to say the word 'kiss' to her.

'I'm sorry I didn't prevent it.' Did she mean the kiss? 'I mean, sorry I didn't warn you to be careful of the food until you got used to it.'

'I didn't mean that. I'm sorry that I—'

'Played that trick on me about the burn?' She still looked straight ahead, her voice pitched higher than usual, as if it took an effort for her to control it. 'Don't worry about that. It was funny. Something my sister and I might have played on each other when we were young. You have a younger brother, don't you? Perhaps you and your brother did something similar. Though maybe not. Boys wouldn't ki— Do that.'

'No. They wouldn't. My brother and I were more for rough and tumble games. The farm was our playground.' No surprise when his brother had grown up wanting nothing more than to take over the family farm. As his father had taken over from his father, Max's grandfather.

So the kiss would be ignored? She obviously hadn't felt what he'd felt when he'd held her close. To her it had been a silly game of no consequence. 'No need for any further apologies, then,' he said. 'On either side.'

'Okay,' she said. Finally she turned to him. He drank in the sight of her face, make-up free, cheeks flushed pink, utterly lovely. How had he thought her eyes were plain brown? Those green flecks seemed to make them appear a different colour each time he saw her. Or maybe that was because he was looking more closely. 'I did enjoy the laughter though,' she said with, he thought, a touch of wistfulness.

'As did I,' he said.

She smiled.

'So we're good, then?' he asked, relieved. He'd felt uncomfortable with her initial chilliness.

'All good. Now hold on, the water gets choppy once we get out past the reef that surrounds the island and onto the open sea.'

The ride did become bumpy with water spurting over them as the boat increased speed. 'This is fun,' he said, exhilarated by the splash of the spray, the thump as the boat rode the crest of the wave then slapped back onto the water. He gave up holding onto his hat and squashed it under the bench. Nikki had tied her hair back off her face but a few stray wisps waved wildly around her head in the wind.

'Better than a fairground ride,' she said, laughing.

Her laughter. It was warm and melodic and engaging. More than anything, he thought, that was what had prompted the chilli kiss. There was something very sensual about shared laughter with a beautiful woman. With *this* beautiful woman.

'Where is this wild ride taking us?' he asked.

'That depends,' she said.

'On what?'

'How competent you are in the water. You may be a champion top-ranking tennis player but I have only your word as to how safe a swimmer you are.'

'I think you can take my word on that.' Max couldn't help but feel affronted. He wasn't used to having his athletic prowess questioned.

'As your guide, I have to make my own judgement on that.' This time when she turned to look at him there was a spark of mischief lighting those extraordinary eyes.

'So you like having me in your power?' he said. Over the sound of the outboard motor and the swishing of the water, he doubted Wayan could hear what they were saying so felt free to skip the pretence they were strangers.

'Whatever made you think that?' she said with what looked suspiciously like a smirk hovering around her mouth.

'Just a thought,' he said, unable to stop an answering smile. Or to prevent thoughts of what it might be like to be in her power in a more intimate way.

'Seriously, I'd be remiss in my duty if I let you just dive in without knowing if you can stay afloat. You'd be surprised how many people tell me they can swim when they really can't. But I haven't lost a snorkeller yet.'

'That's reassuring,' he said with as good grace as he could muster. She was only doing her job— though how she'd ended up in a job like this was beyond his comprehension. From all reports she had been a supercharged CEO of her own company, with a business degree to boot.

'We're heading for the mangroves at the other end of the island,' she said. 'You know the island is only four kilometres long, right?'

'I cycled down to the mangrove forest yesterday,' he said.

He'd taken a boat ride through the quiet, dark waterways under the overhanging mangrove trees and passed the exposed roots that reached into the clear water. It had had an eerie peacefulness. Sitting by himself as the boatman had punted them along, again he had been struck by his aloneness.

The driven life of a professional tennis player had been followed by the rigid regime of rehabilitation. He'd been so determined to prove the doctors wrong and restore his career it had left room for nothing else—not even a flirtation with a cute physical therapist who had made her interest obvious. Looking back, he saw all the activity had masked the essential emptiness of his life.

Yet his solution was more control—timetables, schedules, goals set out and achieved. Control over himself, control over his time, control of the people he'd gathered around him to ensure he was the best he could be. One goal attained, another to reach for, no room in his life for someone to share it with him.

'Don't leave it too long to get hitched, son,' his father had said on his last visit. 'We don't want to be doddery old grandparents.' But marriage and a family of his own were still on hold as he determined a new future. He had loved Ellen, his tennis player girlfriend, but it hadn't been enough to keep them together when it had come to conflicts in their tournament and training schedules. When they'd broken up he'd played the worst tennis of his career—a fact noted by the sports media.

'We're heading for Mangrove Point,' said Nikki. 'The spot on the reef where we're taking you has a gentle current and is a great introduction to snorkelling off Nusa Lembongan.'

'And then?'

'If I think you can handle it, we'll take you to Crystal Bay around on the larger island of Nusa Penida.'

'So, baby steps first,' he said.

'If you put it that way.'

Max went to protest that he didn't need babying but he swallowed the words. Actually he didn't really care where they went. He was back in Nikki's very enjoyable company and out here on a small boat on a big sea they were about as private as they could be.

'How did you end up acting as a guide?' he asked.

'I lived in Manly on the northern beaches until I was a teenager and never far from a beach after that. I loved the sea—swimming, surfing, snorkelling. When I was old enough I learned to scuba dive. The first thing I did when I got here was dive the reef and I totally fell in love with the place.'

'Swimming on the reef is one thing. Taking people out as a guide is another.'

She shrugged. 'It's temporary, isn't it? Like a vacation job really.'

'That makes sense,' he said.

'I was too distraught the first few days I got here to do much but go out snorkelling or curl up in my room. Either activity meant I didn't have to talk to people. That eventually passed and I began to take note of what was happening here.'

'You mean with your friends' venture?'

She nodded. 'I could see Maya and Kadek had done an amazing job renovating and rejuvenating the hotel. They built the wonderful villas we're staying in to extend the range of accommodation. But there were a few areas where they could generate more revenue. Guests wanted to snorkel or dive or take a trip around the island. They'd just refer them to the existing businesses. My friends were too flat out with getting the buildings up to scratch to cut deals with operators and book them through the hotel, or even keep good boatmen and guides on retainer. I thought maybe they could build up to having their own dive shop attached to the hotel one day, buy their own boats.'

'Ever the business person,' he said. *'Sydney's energetic entrepreneur, Nikki Lucas'* was a common label applied to her in the media.

'My father says it's in the blood.' She smiled. 'I'm not so sure about that but if I see a way to make money—honestly, that is—I want to chase it. Luckily, Kadek didn't think I was interfering and welcomed my advice—not that he didn't have plenty of good advice from his own hotelier family, of course.'

'Has it all worked out?'

'So far, really well. They organised things in their own way, keeping staff and family on board. I'm happy to fill in as a guide when required.' She gestured around her to the glorious water sparkling and dancing in the morning sun, the large volcano over on Bali, Mount Agung mysteriously shrouded in cloud in the distance on the mainland. 'How could you possibly call this work?'

She looked up at him, her face shining with enthusiasm and a kind of joy that warmed Max. He wished he could have more quiet time with her. He'd like to bounce some of the ideas he'd had for his future off her. He'd like to— *No.*

Sitting so close to her, her curves accentuated by the tight stretch fabric of her swim shirt, her slender, bare legs so tantalisingly close to his, he couldn't let his thoughts stray to kissing her— properly this time—holding her, making love to her. Not when they were so scandalously linked they couldn't afford to be caught together. Not when he had nothing to offer her in the way of a relationship. Nikki was so obviously not a no-strings-fling kind of woman. And that was all he had to offer at this time of his life, retired from tennis and determined to focus on the transition from the man he used to be to the man he wanted to be now.

Not that she'd shown any such interest in return.

'Not work at all,' he said. 'Unless you find I can't swim and you have to save me from drowning and give me the kiss of life and—'

She raised her eyebrows, but a smile danced around her lips. 'Really? I can see where this is going and I—'

At that moment, Wayan shouted something from behind them. The wind caught the boatman's words and Max couldn't make out what he'd said.

But then Nikki pointed past the starboard side of the boat. 'Dolphins!'

All attention was then on the small pod of frolicking dolphins just a few metres away from the boat. And he never did get to hear where Nikki's thoughts on giving him the kiss of life—any kiss—were going.

CHAPTER SIX

NIKKI KNEW IT was probably a waste of breath to suggest that Max keep on his life jacket for his first foray into the water at Mangrove Point. But she felt obligated to do so.

'No. Flat out *no*,' he said. Then scowled in masculine outrage. 'I'm an Aussie, Nikki. We swim. You know that. I was swimming in the creek at the farm when I was three.' About the same time he'd first picked up a tennis racket, she remembered reading.

'I know,' she said. 'But some people freak out when it comes to swimming in deep water in the open sea.' And more people than she would have imagined—even Australians—either couldn't swim well enough to handle themselves in the sea or couldn't swim at all.

'That isn't going to be me,' he said emphatically as he took off the life jacket and tucked it under the bench. He pulled his white T-shirt up over his head, leaving that magnificent chest bare, just touching distance away from her. She caught her breath, mesmerised by the play of his muscles beneath his smooth, tanned skin even as he made the simplest movement. Like reaching into his kit bag to pull out his snorkelling equipment. *The guy was built.*

'Look, I can even put on my mask without any help, snorkel too.' He proceeded to put on his mask with great exaggeration and a running commentary that made her laugh.

'I concede you're a master at putting on your mask,' she said. A smile tugged at the corner of her mouth as she pulled her own mask over her head and secured it in place over her eyes and nose.

'While you, however, need help with yours,' he said, with a distinct note of triumph. 'You have some of your hair caught up in it. That will stop your mask from getting a good seal and salt water will leak into your eyes.'

'I was going to fix that,' she said in protest.

Too late.

He reached out to tuck the errant lock away from her forehead where it had tangled near the straps. 'Ouch,' she said.

But it didn't hurt. In fact she had to close her eyes at the pleasure of his touch, his fingers firm and gentle as he proceeded to straighten and adjust the strap.

How could something as mundane as helping a fellow swimmer with her mask turn into a caress? Did she imagine that his fingers lingered a touch longer than necessary, brushed across her cheek tantalisingly near her mouth? Did it thrill her because she'd been so long without a man's touch? Or was it because it was *his* touch?

Sadly, she thought it had everything to do with Max and how attractive she found him. What red-blooded woman wouldn't swoon at this gorgeous man's slightest touch? She was no more immune than the fans who'd voted him to first place in those 'sexiest man alive' polls. Only she was fortunate enough to be in close proximity to him.

For a moment—for a long, fervent moment—

she wished they'd met some other way so they'd be free to pursue at the least a friendship. But even that, if detected by the media, could draw the kind of attention neither of them could bear to endure again.

'Th…thank you,' she stuttered.

'My pleasure,' he said.

How crazy, here they were both wearing masks that covered half their faces and smiling at each other. It would be comical if she weren't finding being so close to him so disconcerting. She needed to plunge into that water to cool off. Pronto.

But first she took Max through some common hand signals used in diving, to communicate both with each other in the water and with Wayan watching from the boat. When she suggested they keep each other near as they swam, Max didn't argue with her. She went to put on her snorkel. And hesitated.

There was something inherently unattractive about the effect of a snorkel on a person's mouth, she thought, as she held it in her hand. Inserting the mouthpiece so you could breathe easily pushed your lips into an extreme pout that she found a tad grotesque. She was reluctant to put hers on in front of Max. A silly vanity, she knew. Ridiculous, really, as it had never bothered her before.

Max had no such inhibitions. His snorkel was on in seconds. He grinned as well as he could around the mouthpiece and didn't look odd at all. Fact was, he was so good-looking it didn't matter. And he was so confident he wouldn't care anyway. She couldn't help a grin in return as she slipped in her own mouthpiece. He gave her the 'okay' signal.

From the side of the boat, she slid into the water and watched Max do the same. She needn't have wasted any worry about his swimming ability. It was immediately apparent he was as competent and confident in the water as she was. As he struck out away from the boat, facedown in the water, she followed him.

As soon as her head was under the water she was lost to any other thought save the wonder of exploring the underwater world that revealed itself to her. Vibrantly coloured fish darted through the coral, the sun filtered through the clear blue water in shafts right down to the floor of the sea, illuminating a waving sea plant, exposing tiny cobalt-blue fish camouflaged against brilliant blue coral. The feel of the water sliding over her skin.

She turned to see Max gliding through the water beside her, arms by his sides to reduce drag, just the kick of his long fins to propel himself forward. Yes, he'd snorkelled before, there could be no doubt about that. She swam alongside him and could see his pleasure in the water, his head turning to follow the path of a shoal of blue-and-yellow-striped angel fish, as he swam in an easy, well-paced rhythm.

Nikki suspected Max was a natural athlete. No doubt good at any sport he tried. Among the best in the world at the one he had chosen to excel at. Who knew what he might still achieve?

As she watched him, he dived down and swam deeper propelled by strokes of his muscular arms, the strength of his powerful torso. He stayed under, holding his breath longer than she could have imagined anyone could—but then as an athlete in peak condition he must have an amazing lung capacity.

On land, he seemed strong and athletic with an insouciant physical presence. His confidence underwater added a further element of gracefulness to his athleticism. His perfectly proportioned body was as streamlined as if he were himself a magnificent sea creature, riding the current rather than fighting it. To her, watching from above, it seemed he belonged there as much as the coloured coral and the sea plants waving gently in the water, the schools of brilliantly coloured reef fish darting in and out of the underwater landscape. He turned and twisted with, she thought, the sheer joy of his physicality.

As she watched him, Nikki felt torn by a yearning to be part of whatever it was he was experiencing. To be with him. She couldn't put a name on what she felt. It ached but it wasn't anything sexual. Or was it? As she watched him glide through the turquoise depths of the sea, the realisation hit her with full force. She flushed, even with the coolness of the water on her face. Yes, she admired him. But not in a dispassionate way. *She wanted him.*

During the time she'd avoided him, her growing desire had pushed insistently against her defences. Defences she'd rapidly put up when he'd held her in his arms as he'd helped her flee from her wedding—and she'd liked it. Liked it too much. That was what all that tingling had been about. Sheer sensual awareness of the best man. She'd taken it for nerves, relief, even embarrassment at the situation she'd got herself into.

The more she'd fought it, the more that desire had pushed to be acknowledged as she'd tried to ignore his presence at the resort. Tried to forget the feelings that had surged through her at his brief, unforgettable kiss. Even pretended she hadn't seen him when he'd crossed her path. When in fact she'd thought of little else but him. Had even found herself on her side of the common wall between their villas alert for sounds of his presence. She'd spent rather too long wondering if he swam in his lap pool in the black swim shorts he currently wore or nothing at all.

Now that dammed-up desire burst through,

shattering her defences and leaving her vulnerable to him, to her awakened needs. She would have to make every effort to mask it. Nothing had changed. They still couldn't be seen to be in any way linked to that old scandal if they didn't want to be splashed all over the media again in such an unpleasant way. How foolish she'd been to even contemplate a friendship between them. Being platonic friends with Max wouldn't cut it for her. Not when she hungered for the physical.

He'd been under the water for so long she realised she was holding her own breath as she watched him. How long had it been, he swimming, she lost in admiration and newly acknowledged desire? She dived down to join him.

As she reached him, he pointed down to a brilliant blue starfish for her to admire then turned. They powered up to the surface together, emerged from the water at the same moment. Blew the water from their snorkels in plumes. He looked around to find her. Even through his mask she could see his exhilaration, the eagerness to share his underwater experience with her. She'd felt the same when she'd first snorkelled here. Her heart skipped a beat at the sight of him; she knew how difficult it would be to pretend indifference to this man. How much fun it had been for her to swim with him, like-minded, matched in their skills. How much more she wanted.

Now, she swam up beside him, removed her mouthpiece so she could talk to him, treading water. He did the same. His hair was slicked flat to his head, dark with water, his eyes bluer than the bluest patch of the sea. She was treated to his most dazzling smile yet.

'Wow,' he said. 'Just wow!'

Wow! Yep. That was exactly her reaction when she saw Max's half-naked body emerging from the water like some gorgeous mythical merman from his enchanted underwater kingdom. *Just wow.*

She had to swallow hard to make her voice sound normal. 'I'm so glad you enjoyed it,' she said, genuinely pleased at his reaction. One of the things she liked about helping out as a guide was introducing people to these beautiful waters and the marine spectacle that lay beneath the serene aquamarine surface.

'Thank you for bringing me here,' he said. 'It was brilliant. Better than any expectation.'

She forced her voice to sound how a swimming guide should sound, impartial yet encouraging. She the guide, he the client. 'Crystal Bay is even better,' she said. 'Deeper water, more coral, more fish, more colour.'

'So I'm being allowed to move up to the next grade?' he said, with just a touch of sarcasm.

'If you put it that way,' she said. 'Obviously, you're a really good swimmer and experienced at snorkelling. But you understand why I had to see for myself. Safety is paramount.'

'I understand,' he said. 'At the time I felt insulted by your refusal to believe me but—'

'Insulted? I didn't mean—'

'I know.' The smile dimmed. 'I guess I might have to get used to people questioning my skills at anything but tennis.'

She frowned. 'I'm sure that's not going to happen.'

'It will. It has. Taking a new turn in life is never straightforward.'

'No, it's not,' she said, thinking of the way her

own life had gone since she'd made that fatal decision in the car on the way to her wedding. How she couldn't stay hiding on this island for ever. How maybe one day she might trust a guy enough to consider a relationship. But not now. And certainly not with a man she'd have to share with thousands of adoring fans who hung posters of him in their bedrooms. A man trumpeted in the media as a love cheat. Much as she might want him. 'But I'm sure with your skills and contacts, you will be successful in whatever you choose to do. I… I'll watch your new career with interest.' *From a distance.*

'I'll keep you posted,' he said politely. But she suspected he didn't mean it. How likely would it be that their very different paths in life would cross again after his two weeks on the island were up?

She looked across to the boat. 'Wayan has put the ladder down so we can easily get back on board. Crystal Bay is quite a way away. We have to go around Nusa Ceningan, which is even smaller than Lembongan, then around to the east coast of Nusa Penida, which is the largest of these three islands. *Nusa* means island, by the way.'

'How did I not know about this fabulous place?' he asked as he effortlessly pulled himself up out of the water and onto the boat.

She averted her eyes from the sight of his gorgeous, near-naked back view. *Eyes off the best man,* she had to remind herself yet again.

Max didn't feel much like talking in the boat on the way back from Crystal Bay. The water there had been everything Nikki had promised. More. As he'd swum in that underwater paradise he had realised for the first time since the accident he had felt happy, relaxed, and living in the present rather than angsting about the past or worrying about the future.

He'd enjoyed a non-competitive sport, swimming with Nikki for fun, not seeing her as a rival he had to beat at all costs. To crush his opponent had been his mindset for so long he'd found it difficult to switch out of it enough to enjoy a sport for sport's sake. That had been his only motivation during the gruelling year of full-time rehab.

To focus both physically and mentally on getting back in shape so he could win again. The pressure had been so intense the knowledge that he wouldn't compete again had led to an immense let-down. Followed by an immediate drive to find a new direction in life that didn't hang on numbers on a scoreboard.

But today he'd forgotten all that. Thanks to Nikki.

Nikki was relaxed, easy-going, non-judgemental. He had soon realised she wasn't a particular fan of tennis, or of him as a tennis player—and he was okay with that. More than okay. She knew of him, but he suspected he hadn't really been much on her radar until he'd turned up as best man for her groom at her wedding. He felt he didn't have to prove anything to her, to be someone he was no longer.

Today they'd slipped into an easy companionship, swimming together, marvelling at the same beauty of the underwater world that revealed itself to them. In sync. Obviously, she was a kindred spirit in the water. And out of it? He had an overwhelming urge to find out.

Now she turned to him. 'Have you done any scuba-diving?'

He shook his head. 'Not interested. I don't want to be fussed with all that equipment. I'll stick with snorkelling where I'm in control.'

'I can see that point of view,' she said. 'However, there are deeper waters around these islands I'm sure you'd love that can best be appreciated by diving. The island is a good place to learn.'

'That rather depends on who my teacher would be,' he said. His eyes caught hers in an unspoken question.

She met his gaze full on, unblinking. 'I can recommend a good dive school.' There wasn't a trace of flirtation in his snorkelling guide's voice. She apparently had no interest in him as anything other than an inconvenient client foisted upon her by a misunderstanding. A happy misunderstanding from his point of view. Obviously not from hers.

'I'll keep that in mind,' he said, determined not to reveal any trace of disappointment. 'In the meantime I want to snorkel as much as I can while I'm here. Can I hire Wayan and his boat to be on standby for every day of my stay? I'd pay the full day fee, of course, whether I use him or not.'

Her eyebrows rose. 'No one has ever asked that before. But I guess it could be arranged. We'll have to ask Wayan.'

'What about my guide?'

She stilled. For a long moment she looked back at him. He was so intent on her face as he waited for her reply he was barely aware of the constant spray, the rhythmic slap of the water on the hull as the boat navigated the rougher waters of the open sea on the way back to Frangipani Bay.

'I'm not for hire, nor can you keep me on retainer. I might go out on the water with you if it suits my schedule. If not I can arrange for a different guide.' There was a distinct chill to her voice that had nothing to do with wind cooling them in their wet swimwear.

'I don't for one moment think you're for hire. I don't know what your arrangement is with your friends who run the hotel. But today has been… special for me. I doubt it would have been that special with another guide.'

'Thank you. I really enjoyed it too. You were great to swim with.'

She hadn't given him any indication that she felt anything at all for him beyond that. Except, perhaps, annoyance that he was on the island at all. Even further annoyance that he had crashed *Mr James's* boat trip. But she was too professional to show it.

He leaned a little closer. Not that he thought Wayan could hear him but it was important his words weren't snatched away by the breeze. 'Nikki. I enjoy your company. I like you.'

She flushed and dropped her gaze, seeming to fixate on her discarded swim fins on the floor of the boat. 'I…er… I like you too.' The flutter of her lashes, the slight stutter made her words sound like a major admission. Max was surprised at the relief he felt. But he could almost see the cogs in her brain wondering where this was leading.

He considered his words. 'This vacation is shaping up to be the best I've had in a long time.'

She looked up. 'That's really good to hear. Maya and Kadek will think so too.'

He shook his head impatiently. 'I don't mean that. Well, yes, I do. The resort is great. The island is wonderful. But what I'm trying to say is that today is all thanks to you. And I want to spend more time with you.'

Her eyebrows raised in alarm. 'But we agreed—'

'Yes, we did. But out here, on this boat, in this water, the media and all the scandal seems so far away. It's like we're operating on a different clock with different rules for the way time passes.'

Jam karet,' she said. '"Rubber time", they call it here.'

'There's a name for it? *Jam karet.'* He rolled the unfamiliar words around on his tongue. Thought about what it meant to someone who had always been ruled by timetables, obsessed with punctuality. Could there be a different way for him? 'That's not a concept that would fit my old life. But here… I get it. Yeah, I like it.'

'Me too. Although I was so strung out when I first got here it took me a while to get my head around a different attitude. Now, I hope I'll take some of that relaxed feel back with me when I return to frantic Sydney.'

'What about we relax our attitude here? Out on the water, actually *in* the water, no one has recognised me—or you. I haven't seen a flicker of recognition from anyone, tourist or local.'

She assessed him through narrowed eyes. 'I think it's the beard. Even in the days you've been here it's grown. You look different. Maybe not to one of your rabid fans, but to a casual observer.' She shrugged. 'As for me, blonde Australian women are a dime a dozen in Bali.'

As she sat next to him, her damp hair a wild tangle, the imprint of her mask still around her eyes and nose, her cheeks reddened by windburn, he had never seen a more attractive woman. 'Women like you are not a dime a dozen *anywhere*, let me reassure you of that.'

That won him a self-deprecating smile. 'Thank you, it's very sweet of you to say so. But *you* being seen here, or *me* being seen isn't a problem. It's if we're seen *together* that there could be trouble.'

'The longer I'm here, the less I'm believing it,' he said thoughtfully. 'This island is hardly party central. Not a place where paparazzi are popping out of the undergrowth.'

'Perhaps not,' she said slowly.

'Maybe it's a good place to spend time with a person you like.'

'I guess it could be,' she said, not sounding very convinced.

He angled himself closer to her, injected a note of urgency into his voice. 'I'd like to spend some time with you, Nikki. More snorkelling, tomorrow perhaps. Maybe lunch today.' He glanced down at his waterproof watch. 'I'm grateful for those nuts and snacks you brought on board with you. But right now I'm starving.'

She sighed and he could see her conflicting thoughts play across her face. 'During those weeks after the wedding I felt ill every time I opened my laptop. The things that were said about me, about you. I wish there wasn't so much at stake if we were to be discovered enjoying each other's company by the media. No matter how innocent it might actually be.'

Innocent. Was that the right description for his feelings towards Nikki? They certainly weren't platonic. In fact, they were growing less innocent each minute he spent in her company. He wanted more time with her, more opportunities to get to know her.

Max wasn't used to giving into impulse or emotion. The times he had let his feelings rule had led him into trouble. The worst had been his reaction to the unprofessional opponent who had been taunting him both on and off court in an effort to break his concentration. He'd escalated from the professional to the personal. The final insult had been a snide comment about the doubt over the paternity of his former girlfriend's child. During that all-important game his sudden surge of anger in reaction to the guy's smirk had made him forget tactics, forget self-control and smash the guy with everything he had—resulting in the injury that had ended his career.

But there was something implacable about this impulse to be with Nikki. Something that urged him not to hold back for fear of possible consequence. That his time here with her was limited and the opportunity to act on that impulse might never come again.

Back there in the water with her he'd felt something he didn't think he'd ever felt before. Not just appreciation of her beautiful body, gliding through the water with effortless grace. Of her spirit, her beautiful smile. There'd been a harmony between them, as if he and she together were meant to be. Now he felt compelled to grab the chance to see if she felt in any way the same.

He found himself urging her to a course of action when only days before he'd been pressing for the opposite. 'If we're discreet. If we're careful. If we both wear hats and sunglasses—like everyone does here anyway—I'm happy to risk a lunch together. Maybe down at the mangrove end of the island. It seems quieter there.'

'I know a wonderful family-run restaurant there,' she said. 'Small, rustic but the food is incomparable.'

'Sounds perfect,' he said. 'Count me in.'

But the tone of her voice led him to believe there could be a 'however' coming and he wasn't wrong.

'However it's a risk,' she said. 'And not one I'm ready to take.'

Something made him wonder if she was referring to something altogether different from the risk of exposure by the media. There was something in her eyes he couldn't read. Wariness? Fear? Surely not fear of *him*?

His spirits plummeted. He hadn't realised how much he was counting on her saying yes. But as he started to plan his next strategy for winning her over, he realised she hadn't stopped speaking.

'But I'll think about it,' she said slowly, weighing out the words. 'I need some time.'

Despite the urge to want to ask her every five minutes if she'd thought about it yet, he and Nikki spent the rest of the boat trip back to Frangipani Bay in silence. He gave her the space she'd asked for. He knew it was a big ask. A turnaround. There was still risk they might be discovered, that his worst nightmare of press intrusion might rear up again. But there was a greater risk of future regret. He had ten days left on this island in near proximity to Nikki. After that it was highly likely he would never see her again.

By the time the boat headed into Frangipani Bay she still hadn't said a word—yea or nay. But he held his tongue. Until they had to slip back into the pretence that they hadn't known each other before this day.

As Wayan anchored the boat in the shallow waters. Max took off his life jacket and handed it to Nikki.

'I need to stay on board the boat,' she said. 'Tidy the life jacket, talk with Wayan.'

'Have you thought about what I said?' He realised he was holding his breath for her answer.

She paused, then slowly nodded. 'Your time on the island is short. I… I think I might regret it if I don't take the opportunity to…to get to know you a little better.'

He let out his breath in a whoop of relief, stopped short of punching the air. 'Yes! Lunch. Now. Nikki, I—'

She put up her hand to stop him. 'Not lunch. But I have a thought for dinner tonight. Don't make any other plans.'

'Right,' he said. Having got her this far, he wasn't going to argue.

'You might get a call from Maya. If so, just do as she suggests.'

He made a mock salute. 'Yes, ma'am.'

She laughed. 'Now, Mr James, I suggest you thank your boatman and your guide for a great day's snorkelling and get off the boat.'

His instinct was to hug her. But common sense told him that would not be the right move. She had met him more than halfway. The next move had to come from her. He thanked both Wayan and Nikki, jammed on his hat, put on his sunglasses, picked up his kit bag of snorkelling equipment and got off the boat. He waded through the water and onto the beach without looking back.

CHAPTER SEVEN

LATER THAT AFTERNOON, Max did indeed get a call from Nikki's friend Maya. She apologised for not having made contact earlier and invited him to come to her house at the back of the resort complex for six p.m. to meet her and her husband Kadek.

Max was intrigued. Was this an invitation to have dinner with them and Nikki? If so, he had mixed feelings. Yes, it was one way of seeing her again safe from the public gaze. But he would so much rather see her one to one. No chaperones. Just him and her. Alone and getting to know her better. Anticipation shivered up his spine. When had he last felt this way about spending time with a woman? Not just a woman. *This* woman.

The friend who had warned him that he might get bored in Nusa Lembongan could not have been further from the mark. Max hadn't experienced a moment's boredom since he had seen Nikki step off that boat and back into his life.

He arrived at Maya's house promptly at six. Although finding himself seduced by the concept of *jam karet*, he wasn't yet won over. Punctuality was deeply ingrained in him. The house sat in its own garden behind the last row of bungalows. He entered through traditionally carved wooden gates into a stone courtyard complete with lush greenery, a water feature and eye-catching Indonesian artefacts.

A petite, lovely dark-haired woman in an elegant, traditionally inspired top and wrap skirt in a batik print greeted him with a welcoming smile. 'Hi, I'm Maya. So pleased you could come.' She introduced him to her husband, Kadek, tall, handsome in a high-collared white shirt over a boldly patterned sarong type garment. In this kind of heat, Max thought, a sarong would be a good idea. He'd always dressed conservatively, never knowing when a photo of him might be snapped by paparazzi. He must ask Kadek about the best type for a Westerner to wear.

'I've been looking forward to meeting you both,' Max said sincerely. Maya had obviously been a true friend to Nikki; that predisposed him to like her.

'We've kind of met before,' Maya said. 'I was one of Nikki's bridesmaids but I couldn't make it to the rehearsal so you might not recognise me.' She spoke perfect English with a distinct Australian accent.

Max narrowed his eyes as he thought. 'I think I remember seeing you getting out of the car with the other bridesmaids at the church. But I was watching out for the bride.' Already the bride had been running late and he'd been edgy.

'You did a great job on rescuing Nikki from that dreadful man. Her friends thank you for that.'

'Uh, yes,' he said, uncertain as to where this was going. *Where was Nikki?*

Maya laughed. 'You're probably wondering what you're doing here. Come on through.'

She and Kadek led Max through to an open living area with a polished stone floor scattered with bright rugs and traditional Balinese wooden carved furniture. But it was the carved wooden settee, piled with colourful cushions, that drew Max's attention.

Nikki sat in the centre, cradling a tiny, dark-haired baby. She looked up to greet him and her eyes were still warm with a doting kind of love that had obviously been directed at the baby. 'You're here,' she said. She got up, baby still in her arms. 'Meet Putu, Maya and Kadek's first-born son.'

Max was reeling at the sight of Nikki looking so at home with a baby in her arms. But as she took careful steps towards him he began to think he was hallucinating. She was wearing the same blue dress as at the rehearsal, as in his recurring dream. Her hair was pulled back the same, only now it was fixed with a spray of white flowers. She was wearing the same silver sandals. And her eyes had that dreamy look of love that was so disconcerting in his dreams. Though the love was for the baby, not for Dream Max. 'Nikki,' he managed to get out of a suddenly choked throat. Why did he feel as if he'd been aced?

'Isn't he cute?' she asked, in a doting tone of

voice that did not completely disguise an under-tone of yearning.

Max cleared his throat. 'Uh, yes. Very cute.'

He hoped she wouldn't ask him to hold the baby. He wasn't used to babies. Didn't know how to handle them. What to do with them. It had to be admitted—babies scared him. In more ways than one. Their unpredictable digestive systems scared him; their propensity to scream blue mur-der if placed in his arms scared him; but what scared him most of all was the effect an un-planned pregnancy could have on a guy's life. His brief legal battle with his former girlfriend had shown him that. Her baby had not been his, but before that had been proven by DNA he'd thought a lot about how he could do the right thing and maintain a relationship with the child.

But little Putu was cute, very cute, with fine black hair and merry dark eyes. 'He's a great little guy. You must be very proud,' he said to Kadek.

'We are,' said Kadek, the warmth in his eyes speaking to the truth of his words.

In fact, each of the other three people in the

room were united in looking adoringly at the baby, eyes glazed with fondness. Secure in Nikki's arms, little Putu chortled with glee at the attention, waving his tiny hands about. Until suddenly he stilled and his face went very red and strained. A symptom, Max suspected, of something alarming happening in that baby digestive system. At one end or the other.

To Max's intense relief, Maya expertly swept the baby from Nikki. 'I'll see to him and be back as soon as I can,' she said.

Kadek made small talk and offered drinks from a tray on the carved wooden coffee table. 'Nikki tells me you enjoyed your snorkelling trip today,' he said.

'Very much so. I can't wait to get out there again,' Max said. But he was finding it difficult to concentrate on what the other man was saying. It was as if everything and everyone were out of focus, the spotlight shining only on Dream Nikki.

'I've seen you in that dress before,' he said, not attempting to hide his admiration. In fact, he remembered almost to the very minute when he'd first seen her wearing it.

The tall woman in the blue dress had caught his eye when he'd got to the church for the rehearsal. She'd been laughing at something an older lady was saying. He'd been struck not so much by how she looked—though he'd thought her very attractive—but what could only be described as her aura of warmth and vivacity. Not that he believed in actual coloured auras that psychic people claimed to see surrounding a person. In fact he didn't believe in anything supernatural of any kind. But there had been something about that girl in the blue dress that had drawn him so his gaze had kept returning to her again and again. He well remembered the intense stab of disappointment he'd felt when he'd discovered she was the bride, about to marry his recently rediscovered 'friend'.

'When did you—?' She answered the question herself. 'The rehearsal. I was wearing it that night, wasn't I? It was so hot.'

She was so hot. And he'd seen her many times in the dress since then in his dreams. He certainly had no intention of telling Nikki that. She'd think he was crazy and run screaming. He wouldn't blame her. Maybe he *was* a tad crazy when it came to her.

How sane was it to suggest they see each other alone when he knew what the outcome could be if they were discovered together by the media? His civil break-up with Ellen had degenerated into enmity thanks to the media casting him so unfairly in the role of love cheat. A reputation further cemented by the 'runaway bride' episode. If the press caught them together again his totally unwarranted reputation as a sleaze would endure. Yet seeing her here, he wanted to be with her more than ever.

'It's a lovely dress,' he said lamely. 'You look, uh, lovely.' What was the matter with him? He was usually not short of a reply, of banter and repartee to keep a social conversation going.

'Thank you,' she said. 'I'm glad you were able to come tonight.'

'How could I not?' he said. Nothing could have stopped him from accepting Maya's invitation.

'If you're willing to take a risk of being seen out together, I can help out Maya and Kadek at the same time. That's what you're here to talk about.'

Just then Maya swept back into the room. 'Putu is in bed and now we can return to adult conversation.' She turned to Nikki. 'You were explaining the plan to Max?'

'I'd just started,' Nikki said. 'Max, you know Maya and Kadek are working hard on making Big Blue an even better resort than it is already. They've made a lot of improvements.'

'But more to come,' said Maya.

'We want to make our restaurant a destination in its own right, not just somewhere for guests to have meals,' said Kadek.

The Big Blue restaurant was in a rotunda-type building right on the beach. Max hadn't eaten there yet—he'd had room service when he'd actually been at the hotel for meal time. Including, of course, the memorable afternoon tea. The food had been consistently good.

Nikki continued. 'Maya asked me to visit some of the island restaurants to check out their new menus.'

'To see if there was anything we could be doing better,' said Maya.

'Maya and I were going to go out together to-night to one of the good restaurants not far from here,' Nikki said.

'Even though there are risks in that,' Maya said. 'I might be recognised as a rival hotelier.'

Nikki directed her words to Max. 'You, how-ever, would not.'

'What better front than a couple enjoying a nice dinner for two?' said Maya.

'While surreptitiously photographing the menu,' said Nikki.

'And taking photos of the plated meals suppos-edly for social media but really to show to our chefs,' said Maya.

'You mean me? Me and Nikki?' asked Max, bemused.

He looked to Kadek. Kadek threw up his hands. 'This is something the girls cooked up.'

'We would be like the secret shoppers they send into stores to check the service,' said Nikki. 'Only we'd also get a really good dinner.'

Her eyes pleaded with him to say yes. Max thought he would do anything she asked of him. 'Sign me up. I'm in.'

'Wonderful,' said Nikki. She and Maya gave each other a high five. Max couldn't help wondering what was more appealing to her, the dinner or his company. He'd take his chance on making sure the pleasure of his company won out.

Maya tucked her hand into the crook of Kadek's elbow and looked up at him lovingly. 'Good. I get to have a quiet night in with my husband.' Kadek put his other hand over his wife's and looked down at her with equal affection. Max felt a stab of something uncomfortably like envy.

What would it be like to have the kind of loving security that Maya and Kadek so obviously shared? As his parents did, even after all their years together? The closest he'd come to the kind of partnership he held as the ideal was with Ellen. But it had never developed past initial high hopes. He wondered if they'd both known deep down that the relationship had no future—that it would always come second to their careers. The break-up had hurt at the time, hurt more when she'd quickly moved on to date and ultimately marry the physiotherapist who travelled with her on tour.

Kadek stepped forward. 'If you're ready to go now, I will drive you both in the truck to the restaurant.'

Max frowned. 'Won't it look suspicious to have us arrive in the truck with a Big Blue logo on the side?'

Nikki shook her head. 'Not at all. It's common to drop off guests to other destinations. The restaurant would send its own truck to get us if we booked it. But we thought that would be drawing too much attention to us.'

Us. He and Nikki having dinner together. No matter the pretext, he was going to enjoy it. 'Okay. Let's do it,' he said.

The Big Blue truck was like the others on the island, open at the back and sides with just a canopy over the top that offered little protection from rain. Luckily the sky was clear. Nikki accepted Max's offer of help to climb in from the rear. Not because she needed it but because, in spite of her resolve to ignore her attraction to him, she couldn't resist the opportunity to enjoy the sensation of his hand on her arm. Even that light, casual touch sent shimmers of awareness through her. It was doubly intoxicating as she now recognised those shimmers for what they were—the stirrings of desire.

Once in the truck, she settled herself on one of the narrow, padded benches that formed the seating. She slanted her legs neatly to the side, aware that her dress easily rode up to expose rather too much bare leg.

'Be warned, there's not much padding on these seats,' she said to Max as he swung himself aboard. She was tempted to offer him a hand up but decided that might be just too obvious. With his athletic build it was very apparent he didn't need help.

'I'm tough,' he said, as he sat next to her at a polite distance.

Tough in body and, she suspected, tough in spirit. He must be to have got where he was in his sport. To be one of the top-ranked tennis players in the world. It was a mind-boggling achievement and she could only imagine the perseverance it had taken him to get there. For the umpteenth time she wished she could get to know him better. Tonight might give her that opportunity.

Kadek was a careful driver, but the roads were narrow with unexpected ruts, and tourists riding motor scooters two or three abreast. They were not long out of the hotel when the truck swerved and Nikki was swung hard against Max. 'Sorry,' she said in that ridiculous way she did when apologising for something for which she wasn't responsible.

He looked down into her face with the slow, lazy grin that made her melt. 'I'm not sorry at all,' he said, his voice low and husky.

They'd been thrown together so closely their thighs were touching. It would be crass to move away. To tug down her skirt from where it had, predictably, ridden up. As if she found his nearness distasteful—which was far, far from the truth. Nikki let her shoulders relax and leaned against him. She realised how long it had been since she'd been as close to a man. But she gave no thought to other men. Just this one. *Max.* She breathed in the scent of him: lemongrass, a hint of cologne, healthy, fit male. Heady. Intoxicating. Dangerously close to arousing.

He made no attempt to move away either. In fact he wedged his legs closer, which kept her from sliding in her seat but also brought them kissing-distance close. 'Where are we headed?' he asked. Did he mean something deeper by that than a question about the truck's direction? *Don't overthink things,* she told herself.

She took a deep breath to steady her racing pulse. Tried to speak normally. Even so, her words came out rather too quickly. 'The restaurant is right on the beach near the most western point of the island. We're passing through the village now. Those beautiful buildings are the temples where families worship. Over there is the elementary school.'

'So you're as good a local area tourist guide as you are a snorkelling guide,' he said, teasing.

'I do my best to excel,' she replied in the same tone.

She spoke with mock modesty but it was true.

Nikki did try to excel at whatever she did. Which was why it was a constant nagging undercurrent to her life that, while she'd succeeded in business, done well with investments, had long-time close friends, she didn't seem to have what it took to succeed in a relationship with a man. Here she was staring thirty smack in the face with nothing but failure—spectacular, public failure in the case of Alan—behind her. No wonder she was terrified of trying again, of ever letting herself trust.

'Is the restaurant far?' Max asked.

'Just a few more hair-raising twists and turns. We should be just in time to catch the sunset.' She was about to say the sunset was very romantic but decided against it. This wasn't a date. They were on an information-gathering mission.

Kadek stopped the truck a short distance from the restaurant. Nikki called a 'thank you' to him then went to get off the back of the truck. Max jumped down first. 'I'm here if you need help,' he said.

'Of course I don't need help,' she said as she prepared to jump. 'I've done this lots of times and—'oh!' She stumbled a little on the uneven ground and landed heavily against him.

'Whoa,' he said as he caught her and steadied her with his hands on her upper arms.

'Th…thank you,' she stuttered.

'You okay?' He looked down into her face.

'Fine,' she said. And feeling finer every second he kept his hands on her arms. His tennis-player calluses felt pleasingly rough against her sensitised bare skin, his fingers strong and firm.

When she didn't move away he pulled her closer, so close she could sense the hammering of his heart, breathe in the exciting maleness of his scent, thrill at the warm strength of his body. She slid her arms around his waist and looked up at him, feeling nervous, excited, uncertain, on the brink of something unexpected. His eyes seemed a deeper shade of blue in the waning light and the intensity of his expression made her breath come short. For a very long moment their gazes locked in what seemed a series of unspoken questions with only one answer. *Yes.*

She was only vaguely aware of Kadek driving away. The world had shrunk to her and Max. Her lips parted in anticipation and she murmured her pleasure when he kissed her. His mouth was firm and warm against hers, his beard surprisingly soft against her skin. She tilted her head so she could more easily kiss him back.

'Is this because we're pretending to be a couple,' she murmured against his mouth.

'No, it's because I want to kiss you,' he said.

'I want to kiss you too.' She licked along the seam of his mouth with the tip of her tongue. 'No chilli this time. You're naturally hot.'

'You think so?'

'Oh, yes.' She wound her arms around his neck and pulled him to her, deepening the kiss. What had started as tender very quickly escalated into something intense, demanding, passionate, so all-consuming all she could think about was Max and the heat they were generating. Desire burned through her. She pressed her body to his as lips and tongues became more demanding.

This. Him. Max. *She wanted him.*

She didn't know how much longer they would have stood there in the middle of the narrow lane kissing, oblivious to their surroundings, if another truck hadn't driven up to deposit visitors to the restaurant. At the sound of its blaring horn, she came plummeting back to reality. Reluctantly she pulled away, immediately had to hold onto Max's arm to steady herself on legs that had turned to jelly. She blinked with bewilderment.

'What happened?' She choked out the words.

Max looked equally shaken. He took in a deep, shuddering breath. 'The inevitable,' he said.

Nikki didn't have to ask what he meant. No matter how she'd tried to deny it, they'd been heading towards this.

'The…the question is where do we go from here?' She knew her voice sounded strained and uncertain.

Max reached out and gently smoothed the strands of her hair that had come loose back off her face. She stood very still, briefly closed her eyes at the pleasure of his touch on her skin. 'Wherever it leads us,' he said.

Could she do that? Could she risk it? The thought was terrifying.

The people from the bus rushed towards them. She and Max stood aside to let them past.

'They're hurrying so they don't miss the sunset,' she explained. 'We should do the same. We need to go.' She went to turn away.

He put a finger under her chin, tilted her face upwards so she was forced to look at him. 'Regretting it already?'

'No. Yes. I... I don't know.'

He released her but then took her hand in his. 'I'm not usually an impulsive person. But I feel compelled to follow where this is taking us—wherever it might be.'

'I'm not sure. I—' She could be impulsive, had used her quick decision-making to her benefit in the past. But feeling like this, about him, was scaring her. *She wanted him too much.*

'We don't have to think any further than tonight,' he said as he looked down into her eyes. 'Just tonight, Nikki. One night.'

CHAPTER EIGHT

THE RESTAURANT SAT by itself on the edge of a small, sandy beach lashed by fierce surf. People at the front tables could wiggle their toes in the sand. To the left were limestone cliffs where wild waves rolled in at all angles and crashed onto the cliff walls. The sunset was glorious, an enormous glowing red orb casting a fiery pathway onto the sea as it slowly sank into the horizon.

Nikki knew the sunsets on this coastline were reputed to be among the most splendid in the world. But she scarcely noticed nature's splendid display. She only had eyes for Max. His face seemed infinitely more interesting. Equally nature's masterpiece. Quite the best-looking man she had ever met. *And hers for tonight.* A thrill of pleasure and anticipation shimmied through her.

She was seated next to him at a table discreetly

set towards the back of the restaurant. While the ones at the very front overlooking the beach caught the best view, the people seated there were also on display. Nikki's choice of table was as private as it could be in the well-patronised, fashionable restaurant. It was just as well no one was looking at them for several reasons, not least of which was that she was entranced by Max and he seemed equally entranced by her.

So much for having to pretend to be interested in each other as she and Maya had planned. The waitress had to ask them twice if they were ready to order—neither she nor Max had even noticed she was there. Such bumbling spies they'd turned out to be. More interested in each other than in analysing the menu and service in the interests of Big Blue. She would have to do better on the spying front. But not just yet. Being with him had suddenly become the overwhelming interest in her world. She kept reliving that unexpected kiss. *Wanting more.*

Max was holding her hand under the table. In fact he'd scarcely let go of it since they'd kissed outside the restaurant. 'How are we going to eat when our meals arrive?' she murmured.

'One-handed?' he suggested. 'You with your right and me with my left.'

She laughed. 'I guess it's possible.'

He leaned closer to her. 'I don't want to let go of you. I have to keep touching you to reassure myself you're still here with me.' There was an undertone of surprise to his words that she totally related to. This thing between them had flared up so quickly. *And could burn out as quickly,* she reminded herself. It wasn't something she could place any trust in.

She entwined her fingers with his even closer. 'I feel the same,' she said, her voice a little wobbly with wonder.

'I have to pinch myself that you actually said that.' He lowered his voice. 'You know, I didn't think you were interested in me at all.'

'I couldn't allow myself to be. Not when we'd been so singed by the scandal I dragged you into. Not when I'd been the bride and you the best man.'

'But now we're two people without ties and—'

'Are you? Without ties, I mean,' she said. 'I wondered. After all, I'm talking to the guy voted sexiest man alive.' How could he be single?

He groaned. 'Don't remind me of that stupid title. I'll never live it down. You should hear what my father and brother have to say about it. There's nothing like the ribbing of two blokes from the bush to keep a guy from getting a swelled head. Though I think my mother was secretly tickled. But in answer to your question, there's no one. Hasn't been for a long time.'

Nikki realised she'd been holding her breath for his answer. She let it out on a silent sigh of relief. 'I see,' was all she managed to say.

'After the accident I was totally focussed on getting fit enough to play again. Obsessed. There was no room for the distraction of dating. What about you?'

'No one. I... I think I'd have to know a guy for ten years before I'd trust him enough to date.' Her comment was meant to be light-hearted but she couldn't help a note of bitterness from slipping through.

His brows raised. 'Really? Ten years?'

She nodded. 'The thing with Alan was that bad. To find out someone I'd believed in had lied to me about something so fundamental caused serious damage.'

Max's other hand went to his nose, once again, the slightly crooked bend showing in the evening light, as evidence of his encounter with Alan's fist. 'Bad for you too,' she said. 'If it's any consolation I think the new-shape nose suits you. It adds a touch of edginess. Make you look even... even more handsome.' She was going to say *sexier* but thought better of it. Not when she was clueless about where this was going. *But she had tonight.*

'I'll take that as a compliment,' he said.

'Please do,' she said. She would like to kiss that nose if she got the chance. Oh, yes, she'd like to kiss him, taste him, explore him. Now that she'd had her first taste of intimacy with Max she wanted more.

The waitress brought drinks, an aptly named sunset cocktail for her, a local beer for him. Still Max didn't let go of her hand and she didn't free it. Instead he demonstrated how well he could pour a beer using his left hand. Picking up her glass with her right was hardly an achievement as she was strictly right-handed. But it was fun. *He* was fun.

'Did you ever see me play tennis on television?' he asked after the waitress left.

'Yes,' she said, wondering where he was going with this. 'I enjoy watching the tennis. And it would have been difficult to avoid seeing you, reading about you. The entire country was behind you when you kept winning those big tournaments. And of course you were so hot you turned a lot of besotted young women onto tennis.'

'The more fans, the better. Good for the game.' It would be false modesty if he tried to deny his celebrity status. She was glad he didn't. 'So when did you first see me?' he asked.

'I think it might have been when you first won Wimbledon.'

'Men's singles. I was twenty-two.'

'I was twenty-one. Finishing uni and starting my own business.' Still with Ray, the high-school boyfriend, thinking they were headed for marriage when he'd been cheating on her for six months with the woman he eventually left her for. Ray, her first big fail when it came to men.

Max let go her hand, made a show of counting on his fingers. 'By my calculation, you've known me eight years.'

'What?' His statement was so audacious, she had to laugh. 'You have got to be kidding me.'

'I could be.' He shrugged. 'Or I could be seriously suggesting you take that first time you watched me on television as our introduction. Eight years ago. Two more years to go before you could trust me.'

'There's something seriously flawed in your logic.' She tried to sound serious but couldn't help laughter infusing her voice.

'Makes sense to me,' he said.

'Except for the fact *you* didn't actually see *me* unless you could somehow beam vision from the centre court at Wimbledon to my house in Sydney.'

He grinned. 'Maybe. Maybe not.'

'I think we'll go with "maybe not",' she said, laughing again. 'As far as I recall, the first time you ever laid eyes on me was at the wedding rehearsal. By my count, that makes nine and a half years to go before—'

He sobered. 'Before you could trust me. Or any other man.'

'That's right,' she said, thinking she'd dug herself into a ditch. 'Though there could possibly be time reduced for good behaviour.'

He leaned closer to her, concern warming his eyes. 'Why, Nikki? Why such distrust? It's not just Alan, is it?'

'No, it's not,' she said, unable to stop a hitch in her voice. 'I had a long-time boyfriend and that didn't end well. A few other disasters when I started to date again. But I don't know that I want to talk about all that. It's a bit heavy for a first date.' She frowned. 'That is, if this is what you'd call a date?'

'It can be whatever you want it to be,' he said. 'I don't much care for labels.'

'We said one night only.' Already the hours were counting down. *One night wouldn't be enough.*

'May I remind you I still have ten more nights on the island after tonight. We could make it ten nights. I can't speak for after that—I don't know where I'll be. It wouldn't be fair to say otherwise.'

'I could be exaggerating about the ten years. But I'm not ready for a relationship. Not sure when I ever will be ready.'

'I'm not in a position to offer one. I don't even know where I might be living. Anyway, "relationship" is just another label.'

'I'm glad you said that. Tag me in a relationship and it's doomed.'

Nikki hated that she sounded down on herself. She was strong, intelligent, had everything going for her. She knew that. But she chose the wrong men. Trouble was she didn't know they were wrong for her until she was already in too deep to easily extricate herself. Perhaps it was because she didn't want to admit she'd made an error of judgement. Or perhaps she was too willing to try and see the best in people and forgive them when she shouldn't. She got that trait from her mother, who had never said a bad word about her duplicitous father, right up to the day she'd died. Given Max's reputation—perhaps he was a mistake too.

'The media, they made a big deal about you and Ellen Trantor. That you…that you cheated on her.'

Max's face set grim. 'I was never unfaithful to Ellen. Ever.'

'That photo…' Nikki hated to dig when it so obviously made him uncomfortable. But she had to know.

'That photo of me having lunch with a female friend was taken after I'd broken up with Ellen.'

'But I thought—?'

'That we were still together? The press certainly took great delight in pointing that out. Fact was we'd split weeks before. But Ellen was facing one of the most important tournaments of her career. She knew the media would make a song and dance about a break-up and asked me to keep it quiet as she didn't want to be distracted from her game.'

'Then they broke the story about your date with the other girl.'

'Which made it look like I was cheating on my girlfriend. Ellen was furious on two counts. The adverse publicity put her off her game and she lost. Then she refused to believe that I hadn't been dating the girl during our relationship. For the record, the girl I was lunching with was an account executive from the sportswear company that sponsored me. There was nothing romantic between us, and there certainly wouldn't have been after that whole thing blew up. As the so-called "other woman" she was hunted by the press everywhere she went, even had paparazzi popping out of the flower beds at her parents' house. She hated me.'

'Wow. I'm sorry. I had no idea.'

His mouth twisted into a bitter line. 'You can see why I despise press intrusion into my private life. That incident cost me several matches, too. I've never played so badly. It also lost me the friendship and respect of Ellen, a woman I had deeply cared for and a peer. Playing against her in a doubles match became a nightmare—every time a "grudge match" according to our media "friends".'

'And that other girl? The former girlfriend from your home town who gave that horrible interview in that magazine?' She shuddered at the memory of those vindictive words.

He grimaced. 'How did I get cast as the villain in that case? I was single, she told me she was single when we met up again on one of my flying visits home to see my parents.'

'You mean you had ex-sex?'

'No strings. By mutual consent. But she couldn't have been single at the time because I was definitely not the father of her child.'

'Yet you got branded as the love cheat?' she asked, puzzled. 'How did that happen?'

'Turns out the father was a guy I'd known at school. Not difficult in a small school in a small country town. The media made out I was cheating on a friend.'

'Then you were made out as doing the same thing with me—the best man betraying his friend the groom. Which was utter nonsense, of course.'

'*All* of it utter nonsense. But the gutter press breeds on creating scandal. That kind of beat-up story gives their readers and viewers a temporary "ooh-ah" kind of thrill. Makes them think they "know" a celebrity. But it changes the lives of those involved and not for the better. Mud sticks. There are people who believe there's no smoke without fire. Each time it's happened to me, people I respected thought less of me.' His eyes were clouded with disbelief that he should have been judged so unfairly for something he hadn't done.

'I think more of you for sharing that with me.' He took her hand again. She tightened her clasp on his hand when what she really wanted to do was hug him and comfort him. 'And I appreciate you want to take a chance on me, in spite of the consequences if we're discovered.'

If the press who hounded him could blow up something as innocent as a lunch date, what might they make of the best man and the runaway bride 'hiding out' on an island six months down the track?

'Why don't we take it day by day?' Max said. 'One night at a time.'

Her heart kicked up a beat. 'Are we talking a fling? A no-strings fling? If so, I've never had a fling. I don't know how—'

'Just another label,' he said.

'So a no-label fling?'

'If that's what you want to call it. But I'd rather forget about labels altogether.'

'No labels…no expectations,' she said slowly.

'Just enjoy each other's company without worrying where it's headed,' he said.

It was a refreshing thought. She'd always worried about where a relationship was headed before it had really started. Here, away from her life back home, could be the right place to take a risk on something different. With a man so very different from anyone she had ever met before.

'Yes,' she said. 'Get to know each other in the time we have.'

'The clock has already started ticking on that time,' he said. 'There's so much I want to know about you. So many questions I want to ask you.' She was surprised at how urgent he made that sound.

'Fire away,' she said. 'I'm ready to answer your questions. Like you answered mine. But there's one thing I want to get out of the way first. I… I haven't been completely honest with you about something important.'

* * *

Dread clutched Max deep in the gut. Just when he was allowing himself to relax into the real-life scenario of being with his dream girl in the blue dress. That kiss had taken his dream a whole lot of steps further from where it usually ended. Nikki. In his arms. Passionate. Exciting. *Real.*

A hundred hideous reasons for Nikki being dishonest with him churned through his brain. He had always placed great store on honesty and trust, even before he'd been played by the press. He let go of her hand, placed his on the table. Immediately felt bereft of her touch. 'What do you mean?' He braced himself for her reply.

'I said I was dreaming up ideas for a new venture. Truth is, that venture is well and truly in the development stage.'

'A business venture? And you didn't tell me that because—?'

Her eyes flickered nervously. 'It's that trust thing again.'

'So why confide in me now?'

'Because I don't think you look at me with dollar signs flashing in your eyes.' She looked down at the table. 'Like Alan so obviously did.'

He was so relieved he nearly gagged. 'Dollar signs are not what I see when I look at you, Nikki, I can assure you.' What he saw was a woman exceptional, not just in looks, but in nature. How could any man let her go? No wonder Alan had whacked him in the nose. Nikki underestimated herself if she thought a man would only be interested in her money. Even Alan must have been hurting at her loss from his life.

'I also think you probably have enough of your own money not to be interested in mine,' she said.

'You're right there. I've been caught too often by people more interested in what I have rather than who I am.'

Nikki nodded. 'Just Max. Not Max the celebrity. Not Max the millionaire. The Max I've got to know and to…to like.'

'Exactly,' he said. 'And I like you for the you I've got to know over the last days. Not just beautiful Nikki—that's a given—but smart, clever, kind Nikki. I can assure you your personal wealth has no interest for me.'

I have more than enough for both of us. Max swatted the thought from his mind. He wasn't thinking of a future with Nikki. He couldn't. He was a single-minded kind of guy. Needed to get his life sorted before he could consider a relationship. He had to be careful he didn't raise expectations of anything he couldn't fulfil. Especially when he was beginning to realise the damage that had been done to her by unscrupulous men in her past. He didn't want to be another man who hurt her.

'So as far as wealth is concerned, we're on an even playing field,' she said.

'And perhaps I've gained a few minutes' credit in the trust department?' he said.

'Maybe even a few hours,' she said with a smile that made her eyes dance.

He wanted to kiss her, but fought the urge. Holding hands under the table was one thing in terms of possible exposure. Kissing in a crowded restaurant was another, even if most people's focus was on the last minutes of the setting sun.

'Tell me about your new venture.'

'Private swimming clubs for women back home in Australia,' she said. 'Since I've been here I've been shocked at the number of people who can't swim but want to enjoy the water or to keep their kids safe. Australian women from various backgrounds who didn't learn to swim for one reason or another but are embarrassed to admit it. I think they'd value a safe, private environment where they could be taught. Not just to swim but to snorkel and dive, even surf. Remember you said to me, "I'm an Aussie, we swim?"'

Max nodded.

'That's not always the case. The Australian statistics on non-swimmers are quite alarming for a country where death by drowning is a real issue.'

He smiled at her enthusiasm. 'Sounds like a worthy idea. But would it be profitable?'

'I'm looking into that.' Her eyes narrowed in an expression of concentration that was almost sensual in its intensity. 'The clubs would be luxurious without being intimidating. Stroke correction as well as beginners' classes for a wider customer base. A health and beauty spa. Branded swimwear. A swim travel company to take post-graduate clients to destinations like Frangipani Bay and Greece and Croatia for fabulous swimming tours.'

'You thought of all that since you've been here?'

'I would never have thought of it otherwise.'

He realised both her ideas for businesses sprang from a desire to help people, a generosity of spirit he admired in her. First her sister with her skin problems and now women who yearned to be able to swim. He could learn from her. His thoughts for his future had focussed on his needs, not the needs of others. Perhaps he needed to rethink that. Could he, after so long focussing on his need to win? Could he ever share his life with someone else?

'How far advanced are you with your plans?' he asked.

'As far as I can be from up here. I'm working through my father's property development company to search out potential sites, talk to architects.'

'You're on such good terms with your father?'

'I haven't always been. We clash. Perhaps we're

too alike. But he and my mother started the company together—she was an interior designer, he a real-estate agent. They started by flipping houses and went on to apartment blocks and commercial developments. The partnership fell apart when he left her for his assistant. But the point is, my mother left me and my sister her shares. So of course I work through the company.'

'You're at a crossroads in your life,' he said.

'So are you,' she said. 'I'm interested in what path you might take after tennis.'

Work. She was talking about work. Did he have to walk that path alone?

He would usually keep such matters very close to his chest. But suddenly he wanted Nikki's opinion, her business smarts and maybe— No. He was *not* seeking her approval. That would imply something he didn't want to acknowledge.

'Okay. The options. I'm tempted by a directorship of a big sporting goods company.'

She nodded. 'Could be a plan. Keeps you in the world of sport and is prestigious. As long as the directorship would be an active role, not just there for them to have you on their masthead for prestige. I suspect you would get easily frustrated by a passive role.'

'You're right about that,' he said. She was both shrewd and perceptive. 'There's also an opportunity with an elite tennis coaching ranch in the US.'

'Might you find it too difficult to be training others when what you really still want to do is to be out there competing yourself?'

'You've nailed it,' he said, shaken at how she seemed to read his mind. It was disconcerting.

'There is another option.'

She smiled. 'Now I hear some excitement in your voice.'

'Excitement and a touch of trepidation,' he admitted.

'Spill.' She leaned a little closer to him.

'Sports commentator for one of the big cable networks. Covering the major tournaments. All around the world.'

'Wow. You've got the knowledge, the screen presence, the personality. I could really see you doing that.'

'But it would involve the kind of peripatetic

lifestyle I've been living since I was a teenager. Perhaps I want to put down roots.'

'Where?'

He shrugged. 'Ideally Australia. It's home and my parents aren't getting any younger. But I've lived in the UK and the US too.'

'It's all very exciting for you, isn't it?' she said.

Not half as exciting as being here with you.

He looked up to see a waitress heading their way bearing a tray. 'I see our starters heading our way,' he said, welcoming the opportunity to change the subject. 'I'm ready to eat.'

'Me too,' she said. 'But we can't touch a thing until I've taken shots with my phone for Maya. We mustn't forget the reason we're here. I don't want to let my friends down.'

Max pretended to grumble. Made to snatch up the little 'fusion' tacos with an Asian filling before she finished her photo. Complained he would faint of hunger if she didn't let him start on the tuna slices with a spicy soy dipping sauce and a wasabi mayo. Told her it was torture to keep him from the fritters.

But he liked her loyalty and commitment to her

friends. Loyalty wasn't something he'd experienced from a female companion. But then perhaps he'd been too focussed on his game to be able to give it in return.

'Okay, we can start now,' she said. 'Sorry to have made you suffer.'

'You don't look sorry at all,' he said. 'I think you enjoyed torturing me.'

'I'm admitting to nothing,' she said with a delightful curve of a smile.

He held back on his hunger. *Ladies first* had been a strict rule at his house when he'd been growing up. He always followed it. At the table. When it came to opening doors. In bed when his lover's pleasure was as important as his own. He watched Nikki as she savoured her tuna, making little oohs and aahs of appreciation and tried not to think of how she would react if he were to make love to her. He had to suppress a groan at the thought.

'Aren't you having any?' she asked, innocent of the not so innocent thoughts that were occupying him.

'Of course,' he said. 'I was waiting for you to go first.'

'Why thank you, I appreciate that,' she said, oblivious to any play on words.

'Try the corn fritters—they're scrumptious.' She caught his eye. 'Watch out for the sambal that accompanies them, though. It's really spicy. I know you don't like it too hot.'

He might surprise her, if he ever got the chance. 'Yes, scrumptious,' he said as he sampled the food. How he wanted to sample *her*.

'What do you think about the restaurant and the menu?' she asked. 'What shall we report back to Maya?'

'I'm no foodie,' he said. 'But it's a bigger menu than at Big Blue, going by their room-service menu.'

'You haven't actually eaten in the Big Blue restaurant?'

'Privacy and anonymity, remember,' he said.

'Of course,' she said. 'Though I don't think anyone has recognised you here tonight.'

'They were too busy taking selfies in front of the sunset to notice anyone else, I think,' he said.

'I know,' she said, rolling her eyes. 'The last time I was here one girl had three changes of clothes for her photographs.'

'Now they're all heads down eating. Which is just what I want to do too. I hope the main courses won't take too long.'

'Be patient,' she said. 'The service is very good here. Another thing to report back on.' He was good at being patient when it came to the food, impatient when it came to having her in his arms again.

The sun had finally slid into the sea and the place was lit by strings of glowing lanterns. The white foam of the surf glistened where it caught the light. Even over the chatter of guests and the clatter of dishes he could hear the water pummelling the cliffs. 'It's very atmospheric,' he said. He'd nearly said *romantic* but caught himself in time.

'It is, isn't it? I might suggest to Maya they invest in some of those lanterns. I really like the effect.'

'It's an impressive menu too,' he said. 'A good mix of Indonesian and Asian food with Western dishes too. People from all around the world come to this island. The variety is excellent. Vegetarian and vegan choices too.'

'It's impressive all right. I notice here they specialise in barbecue foods. I wonder if Big Blue should specialise to make their menu stand out.'

'Desserts,' he said immediately. 'Really fabulous desserts. That would draw the punters in, I reckon.'

Her eyes widened. 'I didn't think of you as a dessert fiend.'

'I had to suppress a lot of cravings when I was training. There's a lot you don't know about me.'

Her eyes glazed over, narrowed a little. 'And I have ten nights to discover it,' she said, her voice low and husky.

Max was too astounded to reply. He wondered if he had underestimated lovely Nikki when it came to the not so innocent thoughts.

CHAPTER NINE

WOULD MAX EXPECT her to go to bed with him tonight? It was all Nikki could think about as she stood shoulder-to-shoulder with him in front of the carved wooden gate to her villa. Surely the thought must be playing on his mind as much as it was on hers? Not to mention the urgent signals her body was sending her. *My needs, remember?*

She wanted him. She *really* wanted him. But she still didn't know him very well and to be intimate with someone who was still virtually a stranger had never been part of her romantic game plan.

She'd always been a commitment type of girl. Admittedly she'd been a schoolgirl at the time but she'd dated Ray for six months before they'd made love—her first time.

Perhaps it was to do with her upbringing by her

religious mother. One of the reasons her mother's last years had been so miserable was because her religion didn't recognise divorce. While in the eyes of the state her mum had been divorced, in the eyes of her church she wasn't. There'd been no thought of a second marriage for her, despite her father having wed his mistress to make her wife number two. Her mum had drummed into both the girls that sex should be part of a committed relationship. Nikki had discovered the truth in that herself. Now she wasn't so sure.

Maybe now was the time to stir up her life a little and do things differently. Take what she wanted without worrying about where it might lead. By agreeing to the no-label fling she'd taken the first step. *With Max.*

Kadek had picked her and Max up at the restaurant in the truck. He'd just said goodnight and was headed back to Maya and the baby at his house at the back of the resort. Nikki listened to her friend's footsteps on the wooden walkway until they faded into the distance then disappeared altogether.

The silence between her and Max seemed to

stretch out for too long—although it was probably only seconds. She became intensely aware
of the sounds of the evening on the warm, tropical night. Birds rustled in the trees above them.
Some kind of insect gave an intermittent chir-
rup. The sea swished gently onto the sand of
Frangipani Bay. There was the distant crow of a
rooster—they seemed to crow without timetable
at all hours of the night. And her own breathing,
too rapid, making her feel faint. Perhaps from the
rich fragrance of frangipani that hung in the air.
Or was it because she was alone with Max for
the first time since that hungry, passionate kiss
had changed everything between them?

It was ridiculous to feel so nervous. She was
a grown-up woman of nearly thirty. Not a star-
struck adolescent. She turned towards him. His
face was illuminated by the lantern above the
gate. He looked very serious and impossibly
handsome. She was awestruck at the thought she
had him in her life, even if the time had limits
on it.

'I…er…would like to ask you in for a nightcap.

But—' She stuttered away into nothing. How did she say this?

Without speaking, Max gathered her into his arms and held her close. It felt so good to be back close to him, his warmth and strength. Her dress swooped low at the back and he stroked her bare skin until she relaxed against him. 'But you're worried I might try to seduce you,' he said, his voice deep and rich and laced with humour, his breath ruffling her hair, his hands warm on her body.

She pulled back within the circle of his arms so she could look up at him. A hint of his endearing grin lingered and his eyes were warm. Her heart seemed to flip over inside her chest. 'How did you know?'

'A lucky guess,' he said. 'Or it could be that I'm learning to read you.'

'Oh,' she said, disconcerted that he could understand what she was feeling without her having to say a word. 'It's not that I'm *worried*. Just… I want to. I want *you*. But it seems too soon. I… I told you I haven't had a fling before. I don't know the rules.'

'No rules, no labels, remember?'

Wordlessly she nodded, bowed her head so she looked down at her feet, feeling awkward and more than a little foolish. If they only had the one night she would probably rush him inside to the bedroom. But it was a big turnaround for her to contemplate sex as part of a fling with no future. She would feel so much happier if she knew him a little better before she took that step. Even though it might be a kind of torture to wait. Even though he might lose interest if she put him off.

He tilted her chin with his fingers so she was forced to look up at him. His eyes searched her face. She could see an undisguised desire in them but also a warmth of understanding that surprised her. *Sexiest man alive.* This man could pick and choose from a waiting list of women who wouldn't hesitate to take their clothes off for him.

'Of course I want to take you to bed,' he said. 'You're gorgeous and sexy and I can't think of anything more wonderful than making love to you, Nikki Lucas.'

She thrilled to hear his words and an answering

desire shimmied through her. 'Me too. I mean, I want to make love with you too. But—'

'When you're ready,' he said.

'It's not that I'm a prude or anything but I—'

He laid a finger on her mouth to silence her. 'You don't have to explain or make excuses.'

'It's just that I've always—'

He followed his finger with his mouth in a brief kiss that left her breathless. 'I tell you what,' he said. 'How about I leave it for *you* to seduce *me*?'

'What do you mean?'

'When you're ready, I'm sure you'll be able to find a way to let me know you want to have your way with me.' He gave an imitation of a wicked leer that made him look more handsome than devilish.

'Oh, I think I could manage that,' she said, laughing. She could already think of several ways. *When the time was right.* She felt instantly more relaxed and happier once he'd taken off the pressure. Pressure, she realised, that was self-imposed. He hadn't tried to push her into anything.

He kissed her again. She wound her arms

around his neck and kissed him back—a long, slow, exploratory kiss. It was a kiss that acknowledged mutual desire, that agreed they both wanted more than kisses and—importantly—that insisted there be mutual respect.

'Are you going to invite me in?' he asked, still holding her close, his breathing not quite steady.

Nikki hesitated for only the merest fraction of a second but it was obviously enough for him to pick up on. 'I'll sit on one sofa and you can sit on the other, look don't touch,' he said.

'That's a plan,' she said, not liking it in the slightest but seeing sense in it.

He put on a woeful expression. 'It's not late and if I go next door I'll only sit out in the courtyard and think of you on the other side of the wall.'

So he did that too? 'Would you really?' she said, wondering if she should admit to doing exactly the same thing, deciding she should maintain at least a semblance of mystery. She most certainly wouldn't admit she fantasised about him soaping his magnificent body in his outdoor shower.

'Of course. Then I might dive into the pool and

wonder if you might be doing the same thing.' If he did that, and she heard him splashing, she'd drive herself crazy imagining it and wondering if he swam naked. Her breath caught. *She wanted to see him naked.*

'You...you could come into my courtyard and swim. Or...or we could sit on the sofas opposite each other as you suggest.'

'Or do both?'

'What about—?'

'I can swim in my shorts,' he said.

He must think she was a real prude if he'd picked up on her thoughts about what he might wear to swim in her lap pool tonight. She wasn't ready for naked just yet. But she wasn't a prude— and she looked forward to showing him that. But not tonight.

She reached into her purse for her key. 'I'd only sit on this side of the wall and think about you if I let you go,' she said. She inserted the big, old-fashioned metal key in the door. 'So please do come in.' He followed her over the threshold.

'Ah, the bliss of the air-conditioning,' she said,

holding her arms up to the chilled air. Even at night it was hot and steamy.

Max looked around him with obvious interest. 'It's just like my villa but the mirror image. Nice to see you've added some personal touches. I like the Balinese puppets on the wall and the prints you've got propped up against the desk.' He picked up one of the framed photographic prints. 'Is this the abandoned seaweed farm near here? The colours of the water are incredible.' She nodded. Tourism was beginning to overtake the traditional industry of seaweed farming. 'And this black and white view of Mount Agung is so atmospheric.'

'They're by a local photographer,' she said. 'I bought some other knick-knacks too, so I could personalise the place.'

'The more I look around, the more I see,' he said.

'I've lived here for six months. The villas had only just been finished when I arrived. It's my home. For the time being at least.' When she'd first come to the island she'd thought she'd never want to go back to Sydney.

She noticed he put the frame back in the precise spot he'd taken it from. 'How long do you think you'll stay up here?' he asked.

'Not much longer. I'll need to be in Sydney to decide on sites for my swim clubs.'

'Are you frightened of going home?' he said quietly.

She felt herself flush. 'Frightened? Of course not. All the fuss with the media will be over. Hopefully the runaway bride is yesterday's news.' But she'd go back to Sydney single. The thought of having to face the dating scene again was not an appealing one. Especially when she'd be comparing every man she met to Max.

'Are you worried about Alan?' he said.

She shrugged. 'Not really. When I first saw you here I thought he'd sent you and I felt fearful. He continued to make threats against me for months after the wedding. Scary stuff.'

Max's hands curled into fists. He cursed in extremely uncomplimentary terms about Alan.

'Don't worry,' she hastened to assure him. 'My father paid him a visit and there have been no more threats. In fact, my sister informed me just yesterday that Alan has recently been seen around town with a wealthy widow.'

'It didn't take long for him to bounce back,' he said, his distaste for his former friend evident.

'Perhaps the ex-wives will warn her off like they did me.'

Max moved towards her, his stance protective. 'Make sure you don't do the warning. I suggest you stay right out of it.'

She shuddered. 'I intend to. I want absolutely nothing to do with that man.'

'But you're worried Sydney might be too small to contain both you and him.'

Again he seemed to read her mind. 'Maybe,' she admitted. 'But I have to suffer the consequences of my own actions, don't I? I was the one who was foolish enough to be taken in by him.'

'But you were also the one who found the courage to leave Alan.'

'I keep telling myself that,' she said, but couldn't help a catch in her voice. 'And I know I have to go home soon.' She headed towards the small kitchen area. 'But here I am, offering you a nightcap and all I'm doing is talking. Beer?'

Nikki carried two local beers and a packet of spicy pretzels into the sitting area, and put them on the coffee table. She sat down on one of the sofas and Max, true to his word, sat on the other facing her. It seemed a vast distance over the low, carved wooden table.

'You look lonely over there,' he said.

'I am,' she said. 'It was you who suggested separate sofas.' She patted the cushion next to her.

He needed no further urging and came over to sit next to her. When he put his arm around her, she snuggled close with a happy sigh. 'That's better,' he said, as he pulled her closer.

'So much better than being on opposite sides of the coffee table and certainly opposite sides of the wall,' she said.

The door to the bedroom was open. The staff had been in to arrange the mosquito net canopy over the traditional carved wooden bed. It was a big, lonely bed and she wondered if she was making a mistake by not taking Max by the hand and leading him in there. 'So, do you want to watch a movie? The Wi-Fi is good here so there's a choice.'

Nikki only offered to be polite. She would so much rather talk to him.

'Why would I want to watch a movie when I can sit here on the sofa with my arm around a beautiful woman?'

She looked up at him and was struck by the admiration in his eyes. Admiration and something more she couldn't put a word to but which might have been longing, yearning even. But she had to be careful not to read into it what she wanted to see rather than what was there. She'd been so easily fooled by Alan. For all her jokes about ten years to trust, she didn't know Max well enough to trust him.

For all his denial of any wrongdoing in those publicised cases, she couldn't be sure he was trustworthy in other ways. If she did have an affair with him—no label, no strings, whatever she might choose to call it—if the press found out and her bad choice was once again emblazoned all over the media for the world to know, she didn't think she could endure it. But she could not admit that to him, to anyone.

But right here, right now, she wanted him and

she wasn't thinking past that. 'When you put it that way…' she said, letting her voice trail away.

'There's something I didn't get to ask you over dinner,' he said.

'Fire away,' she said.

'You once told me that Alan knew how to play you,' he said.

'Yes. He was a master manipulator.' And how gullible she'd been to be taken in by him. Would she ever be able to trust her judgement in men again?

'You said something like he made you believe everything you most wanted in life, he wanted as well.' Max's gaze connected with hers. 'So after everything, what is it that you most want from life now, Nikki? I'm really curious to know.'

Max was surprised at how the shutters seemed to come down over Nikki's face, blanking her expression. She edged away from him on the sofa so she was no longer touching distance.

'If I tell you, will you promise not to run screaming from the room?' she said. If she was attempting humour, it fell flat.

'I can't ever see myself running screaming from you under any circumstances,' he said.

'You might change your mind when you hear what I have to say.' Her eyebrows lifted. 'Seriously.'

'I very much doubt it. Don't keep me in suspense.'

'Okay. The truth is, I still want what I wanted then. And what I most wanted was to be married and starting a family before I was thirty,' she said.

He knew he shouldn't be surprised. She'd alluded to that a few times. But not stated so bluntly.

'No chance of it happening now as I turn thirty in September,' she continued. 'But when I met Alan it was feasible.'

'Okay,' he said cautiously, not sure where she was going with this. 'And he said he wanted that too?'

'I told him after our first few dates.' A black mood descended over Max at the thought of Nikki dating another man. He had to shake it off. He had no right to be jealous.

'That was my dating policy,' she said. 'There was no point wasting time with a man who didn't want what I wanted.'

'Like other guys you'd dated?'

'Yes. You might be surprised at the number of commitment-phobic men there are in Sydney. Maybe everywhere in the world, according to my girlfriends. An epidemic of men just wanting to have fun.'

Max hated the cynical twist to her mouth. And yet, could he not count himself among the commitment-phobes? Not for ever. One day he wanted all that. *Just not now.*

'But Alan didn't run screaming?'

'Far from it. He seemed delighted to meet a woman who wanted a family as much as he did. Reminded me of my advancing age. Suggested we get married as soon as we could, while I was still fertile. Of course, he didn't mention he'd had a vasectomy.' She twisted her face into a mock comic expression but didn't manage to disguise the hurt in her voice. *Was she completely over her former fiancé?*

'We all know what a pack of lies that was,' she

continued. 'I would have had a family quickly all right—stepmother to his twins. Those poor little kids having a father like him. How I despise him.' *Guess that gave him his answer.*

'You didn't ever meet a man who shared your views?'

'I didn't actually date enough to find out,' she said. 'Between the time I broke up with the long-time boyfriend and the time I met Alan, I was working insane hours establishing my business.'

'What happened with the long-time boyfriend?' he asked. He hated the thought of lovely Nikki with some other loser who'd wounded her. But he had to know.

'We met in my last year of high school. Lasted all through uni. I actually thought he was "the one". We were unofficially engaged for years.' She paused. 'Are you sure you want to hear all this? It was years ago now.'

'Yes,' he said. He needed to know what made her tick. He'd always made it his business to thoroughly research an opponent to give him any advantage. Not that Nikki was an opponent. Fact was, she fascinated him.

'Okay,' she said. 'Cracks started to show around when I started the business. He didn't like the idea I was more successful than he was, I think. I lost count of the number of times we broke up and then got back together and plastered it all over.'

'What happened in the end?' he said through gritted teeth.

'I was looking at engagement rings while he was cheating on me.' She said it so matter-of-factly, yet it must have hurt like hell at the time. 'I discovered she wasn't the first. He confessed his first infidelity was when I was mourning my mother. Didn't give him enough attention at the time, I suppose.' She shrugged but he could still see tension in her shoulders. 'Worse, he got the last woman pregnant and married her, not me.'

'Your first lucky escape, by the sound of it,' he said.

'I can see that now,' she said.

'And I can see where your ten-year trust again thing comes from,' he said.

'You get a few more hours' credit for recognising it,' she said, in a dismally failed attempt at humour.

'Thank you,' he said, gathering her into his arms again, breathing in her closeness, the scent of the flowers in her hair. 'Please note that I haven't run screaming from the room.'

'No need to worry with a no-label fling is there? We've both been honest about what we expect from the time we plan to spend together. Both realise it can't be more than that.' She kissed him, her mouth sweet and tender on his. 'Besides, I might have to rethink what I want from life. By the time ten years rolls around and I trust some-one enough to consider marriage, I'll be head-ing for forty.'

'Women have babies in their forties.'

'I guess,' she said sounding doubtful. 'I think my only babies are going to be my businesses.'

He went to protest but she spoke over him. 'Look, can we not talk about this stuff any more? Now you know all about my dismal dating past and I don't particularly want to rehash it. Right now I'd rather look to the future than the past.'

'Meaning?' he asked.

'Meaning you've got Wayan and his boat on a retainer for the rest of your stay. I happen to have the day off tomorrow but I'm happy to be your guide if you'd like that.'

'I'd like that very much,' he said.

She smiled. 'Good. I thought maybe some more snorkelling and perhaps we could take a kayak out, just the two of us, currents permitting. That can be a lot of fun.'

Just him and her in a minimum of clothes alone together out on the sea? 'I can't wait,' he said.

CHAPTER TEN

THERE WAS SOMETHING very sexy about secrecy, Nikki thought as next evening she sounded the door chime to Max's villa. 'Room service,' she called in her most official voice, trying not to give the game away by laughing at the surreptitiousness of it all. Anyone passing by would see a staff member. Nothing suspicious.

The night before, she and Max had discussed how they still needed to be circumspect about being seen together. It was important to both of them to avoid any kind of adverse publicity. Behind the high walls of their villas seemed to be the best option for privacy. Hats and sunglasses when they were out in public. The pretence of her as staff and he as 'Mr James' at other times.

She was wearing the hotel's traditional style uniform and bearing a large covered tray containing dinner from the restaurant. One of the girls in the kitchen had remarked that it was a lot of *mee goreng* for one person. In response she'd laughed and said Mr James must be very hungry. After all the exercise she'd done throughout the day she was hungry and was glad he had ordered for big appetites.

Underneath her modest clothes she was wearing her favourite pink bikini. The previous night she and Max had never got around to swimming in the lap pool. In fact they had drowsed off together on the sofa. She'd awoken, startled, in his arms at the same time he had. Just as he'd done on the day of the wedding, he'd picked her up, then carried her into her room and laid her on her bed under the mosquito net. He'd kissed her and left. She'd drifted back off to sleep feeling, safe, happy and something not at all expected from a no-label fling—cherished.

Not that she read anything into that. Max was a gentleman—he'd shown that from the beginning in spite of his reputation. He liked her. He desired her. He was honest about his intentions.

As far as she could ascertain, he was not pond scum. That was all there was to it.

She'd woken up alone, happy she'd made the decision not to invite him into her bed before she'd got to know him better. A perfect day had followed, snorkelling in a different spot at Crystal Bay, lunch at a quiet table in an out-of-the-way *warung* at the mangroves end of the island, followed by taking out a double kayak in the waters around Frangipani Bay and around to the next beach. She couldn't remember when she'd had more fun. She'd done all those things before. But being with Max had made them magical.

The door opened. Max stood before her, framed by the doorway, clad only in a sarong slung low on his hips and that winning smile. Nikki was struck speechless, all the breath knocked out of her body.

The sarong was in a Balinese *ikat* print in multiple shades of blue and contrasted with his smooth golden tan. Blue eyes, blue sarong and a whole lot of muscular male perfection in between. With a hungry gaze she took in the sight—broad shoulders tapering to narrow hips, his hard defined belly, the rippling muscles in his torso, the strong arms that had powered his killer tennis game, and seen them surging through the water in the kayak earlier that day.

Yes, she'd been with him all day when he'd been only wearing swim shorts. But that was for swimming. This was altogether different. This was…more naked somehow. *Was he wearing anything under that sarong?*

'What do you think of the sarong?' he said. 'I bought it from the hotel store. Kadek advised me on how to tie it.'

She swallowed hard. 'You look hot.'

He frowned. 'Do I? The idea is that a sarong is cooler than shorts or trousers in this climate.'

'I didn't mean that kind of hot.' She could feel her eyes glazing over. If she wasn't holding the tray she thought she might simply swoon and fall at his feet.

'I'm glad you think so,' he said. 'It's a guy thing in this country but not where we come from. I was concerned I might look ridiculous.'

'Not ridiculous,' she said. 'Very…very manly.' She had to clear her throat again. 'If they put a photo of you looking like that on a poster for your fans it would sell out.'

'Thank you. But I'd rather keep my new look just between us,' he said.

'Me too,' she said. A sudden possessive urge swept over her. *She wanted him all to herself.*

If she just undid that one knot at the front, would she see the sarong fall away from him? Perhaps it was as well that her hands were firmly clenched on the tray.

'Let me take that from you,' he said, taking the meal from her. He inhaled. 'Smells good.' He carried it through to the circular dining table in the living area.

Then he turned to her again, put out his arms. 'I'm glad you're here,' he said. 'And not just because you come bearing food.'

She laughed and went willingly into his embrace. All she wanted was to be close to him, to be near to him, to be kissed by him. She couldn't let her thoughts stray further than that.

She put up her face for his kiss and a few blissful moments followed. How could she ever imagine sharing such a thing with anyone else?

Excitement built as the kiss intensified. *Take what you can, while you can,* she urged herself. Spending all day together had accelerated the 'getting to know him' process. Too well. It had been a wrench when she, as guide, had said goodbye to 'Mr James' on the beach. In just the few hours since, she'd missed him with an intense sense of loss. Maybe it was time. Maybe tonight.

'Today was one of the best days of my life,' Max said, his voice deep and husky.

Nikki's heart gave a little lurch at his words. Being with him, enjoying the same experiences, laughing with him. His presence nearby had added such a wild joy to the day she'd found herself wishing it would never end. Had he felt the same about her?

'It was for me too,' she murmured. What if he didn't mean being with her at all? What if he'd been referring to the water and the weather? She stepped back from him. 'Yes, it was a perfect day,' she added hastily. 'Those beautiful fish, the coral, the lunch and—'

He reached for her, swivelled her so he could look deep into her face. He traced his finger down her cheek. 'All that. But it was the company that made the day. Being with you, Nikki. That's what was so special for me. You.'

An unreasoning hope soared to life in her heart at the expression in his eyes. 'Thank you. For me too. I mean you. Your company. I... I can't remember when I last enjoyed a day as much.' *Enjoyed a man as much.*

But she couldn't let herself think that this was any more than two people thrown together by circumstance with limited time on a beautiful holiday island. She forced her voice to sound steady. 'You're a mean hand with a kayak. All that upper body strength. You did all the work. I scarcely had to paddle.'

'We were in perfect rhythm together.'

'Yes, we were,' she said, feeling a little breathless. Within minutes on the kayak they'd found their rhythm with the double-bladed paddles, in sync with each other, propelling through the sparkling aqua water in perfect harmony. Even when they'd hit one of the notorious unpredictable currents they'd worked effortlessly together to get the kayak out of trouble. Of course her thoughts had wandered to how their rhythm might match under other circumstances. After all, she was a red-blooded female with needs clamouring to be acknowledged.

'I missed you,' he said, tracing her lips with his thumb.

'It's only been a couple of hours.' She couldn't show how affected she was by his touch, by his words. *She didn't trust this feeling.*

'Those couple of hours away from you seemed very long.' *Was this genuine or a practised seduction?*

'I missed you too.' The words blurted out despite her best efforts to hold back. 'I... I've been counting down the minutes until I saw you again.'

'The wait seemed interminable. But I couldn't very well storm in next door and drag you in here.'

Why not? she thought. It might make it easier for her if he kissed and caressed her senseless until she thought of nothing but making love with him. But she wouldn't want to feel overwhelmed by caveman tactics. 'I... I guess not,' she said.

He looked unbearably appealing in that sarong.

Sexiest man alive and then some. Because of her reluctance he was waiting for her to make the first move. *Her call.*

Was now the time? She didn't know how to deal with this. Nothing had prepared her for the way she felt about Max. Why couldn't she allow herself to look at sex simply as an appetite to slake rather than something special to share between two people who cared about each other? What had she got herself into by agreeing to the no-label fling?

She couldn't let him read those thoughts on her face. Instead she took the few steps over to the table and took the cover off the tray. 'What have we got here? *Mee goreng*—my favourite, thank you.'

He walked over so he was behind her, looking over her shoulder. Too close for her to be able to keep a clear head. All that bare skin and muscle with nothing but the light cotton of her top between them. 'I remembered you said you liked it,' he said.

'And *tom be siap*, steamed chicken wrapped in banana leaves with a lemongrass salsa. That's yummy too. So is the tuna *bakar*—it's a grilled tuna fillet with a spicy Balinese sauce. You chose well.'

'They all sounded good,' he said. 'I was hungry. All the swimming and kayaking today. I thought the kayaking might have made my damaged arm ache but it didn't.'

'That's good news. I'm glad.'

He put his hands on her shoulders and turned her halfway towards him so there was no escaping his gaze. 'For the first time in a long time I feel relaxed. Able to think clearly about the decisions I have to make. It's like I've turned some kind of corner. Thanks to you, Nikki.'

She picked up a fork and started to pull apart the banana leaf wrapping from the chicken. Anything but look at him. 'Any good guide would have done the same,' she said, purposefully misunderstanding him. She'd felt it too out there with him. The magic. The happiness she'd felt at being with him. At playing at being a couple. Struck in unguarded moments by an inexplicable longing for it to be real.

'That's not true and you know it,' he said. 'It was more than that.'

Again her heart gave that painful lurch. It would be only too easy to develop feelings for Max. But she couldn't allow that. He'd made it very clear he wasn't looking for a relationship. She had only just recovered from the emotional fallout from her failed engagement. She couldn't let herself fall for a man who only wanted a fling.

She screwed up her eyes in a kind of despair. *Don't let yourself fall in love with him, Nikki.* She could lie to herself all she liked but she knew she was in serious danger of losing her heart to this man.

She looked up at him. 'We're away from home, in an exotic environment. Both escaping trauma of a kind. It would be easy to think there's more to some vacation fun than there really is.' She was trying to talk herself into believing that as much as she was him.

'You can say that,' he said, his voice controlled. 'That doesn't stop me from believing it was an exceptional day and that the reason it was exceptional was the company of a wonderful woman.'

* * *

Max tried to sound on top of the situation but inside he was in turmoil. Things with Nikki were not going as planned. He had intended a no-strings vacation affair. Something warm and sexy and fun that would help them both heal from the calamities that had driven them in their own separate ways to this island.

It should be something easy to walk away from at the end of his time here. He had his farewell speech prepared—something along the lines of it would be awkward to stay in touch. They both had lives to get back on track. No point in trying to prolong something that had a limited life. No need to exchange phone numbers.

Trouble was, it wasn't turning out like that. *He was falling in love with her.* Head over heels and so rapidly he could hardly keep his feet on the ground. Or that was how it seemed.

It wasn't what he wanted. Not now. Not even in the foreseeable future. Not when he was forging a new post-tennis life. When he got married, he wanted all his ducks to be in a row so he could have the kind of relationship his parents had. One that lasted. Where he would be there for his wife and children. Not absent. It hadn't just been conflicting training schedules that had ended his relationship with Ellen. It had been what she had called—what she had screamed at him when she'd ended it—his absence both physical and emotional.

Truth was, the career he'd striven for most of his life had defined him. He was used to being a champion. A winner. He needed to be back on top with whatever new path he chose before he could ask a woman to share his life.

Nikki could be the right girl at the wrong time. *Perhaps he should back off.*

Although it was hardly likely that she reciprocated any deeper feelings. In fact she'd just given him a nice little lecture about how he shouldn't mistake a vacation fling for anything more significant. He should take heed of her advice. Hope like hell she hadn't read anything deeper into his compliments about how much he'd enjoyed her company.

And stop speculating whether that was a pink bra or a pink bikini giving him tantalising glimpses of the top of her breasts through her lacy white cotton uniform top.

'This dinner will be getting cold if we don't eat it soon,' he said. 'Do you want to eat inside or out in my courtyard? There are citronella candles to keep mosquitoes at bay.'

'The courtyard, please,' she said. 'Do you mind if I change into my swimsuit first?'

No, I'd rather you stayed completely covered up so I'm not tempted by your lovely body. 'Sure,' he said. 'Whatever is most comfortable for you.'

Would she do a striptease in front of him? If so, might he offer to help her undress? First that lacy blouse slid over her shoulders and breasts, then the long skirt, sliding it down over her legs and—

'If you'll excuse me for a moment, I'll pop into the bathroom to change,' she said, heading in that direction.

He suppressed a groan of frustration, turned it into an awkward cough.

'You okay?' she said, turning back.

'Chilli fumes wafting up from the food, making me cough.' He faked another cough. 'Nothing to worry about. You just go.'

'Are you sure? I've seen how chilli can affect you.'

'I'm *okay* with the chilli,' he said, tight-lipped. Would he ever live down that earlier incident? 'You go. I'll unpack the food.'

Just minutes later she came out wearing just a pink bikini top and an orange-and-white-striped hotel towel wrapped around her waist. It stopped short of covering her legs. 'I hope you don't mind if I borrowed a towel,' she said.

Lucky towel. 'Of course not,' he said through a suddenly choked throat that had nothing to do with chilli fumes. Did she realise how artlessly sexy she looked?

'I feel much cooler now,' she said, stretching up her arms so her breasts threatened to fall out of her bikini top. 'That long-sleeved blouse is actually quite warm when it's this hot.'

She was hot. He hadn't seen her before with so little clothing—she wore a sun protective swim shirt out on Wayan's boat. In the kayak she'd worn leggings and a life jacket. Now, the triangles of the bikini top drew attention to the swell of her breasts as much as covered them, emphasised the shadow of her cleavage. Her body was lithe and strong—her slender waist, the flare of her hips, her firm, finely muscled arms in perfection proportion. The more he saw of Nikki, the more he wanted her.

But that was all it was. A healthy sexual attraction. A friendship of sorts. Not anything more. *Of course he wasn't falling in love with her.*

She sat down in the chair opposite him at the outdoor bamboo table and served herself her favourite noodles. 'You didn't order dessert?' she asked.

'Nothing really appealed,' he said. 'I've ordered the caramelised bananas a few times already.'

'I told Maya what you suggested about spectacular desserts. She agreed. In fact she's organised a meeting with her chefs to discuss a new dessert menu. She said to say thank you for the suggestion.'

'She's so welcome,' he said. 'Can you tell her I'm volunteering to taste any new dishes?'

Nikki laughed. 'I'll pass that on.' She sobered.

'Although it's likely that will be happening after you go home.'

'Shame,' he said. Truth be told, he hadn't been thinking that far ahead. Without being consciously aware of it, he had abandoned timetables completely and given in to 'rubber time'.

'Don't worry, I'll send you photos to drool over and...' Her voice trailed away. There had been no mention of any future contact between them after the eight remaining nights. She flushed and looked embarrassed. 'Or...er...not.'

'I'd like that,' he said. But he knew his voice came out sounding half-hearted.

The sudden silence between them stretched out too long to be comfortable, even taking into account that they were eating a meal. She was the first to break it. 'I have news,' she said. 'A very good friend of mine might be coming to the island tomorrow.'

Her news came from left field. 'A friend?' *Male or female?*

'Yes. Sammie and I go way back to high school. She's friends with Maya too.'

Suddenly his wariness about being seen with

Nikki returned in full flood. 'Why might she come to the island?'

'First and foremost to catch up with me and Maya. But she wants to write a profile on me. She—'

Max got up from the table, pushed his chair back so hard it fell over, clattering on the paving. 'She's a journalist? You're inviting a journalist here? After all we went through with the media?'

Nikki got up too, not one to let herself be put at a disadvantage. 'She's not *that* type of journalist. Sammie writes for one of the weekend newspaper magazines. She's in Bali for a short holiday. But Sammie being Sammie never switches off. Her boyfriend is a photographer, he's here with her and—'

'A journalist *and* a photographer? What are you thinking?'

Nikki frowned. 'Sammie is one of my oldest, dearest friends. Another of my bridesmaids. I trust her implicitly.'

'What if she sees me here? What if she puts two and two together? Is that what you intend to—?'

'No! Sammie is writing a feature about me as

an Australian female entrepreneur. About how one of the biggest cosmetic conglomerates in the world purchased my company that was born as a little, underfunded start-up in Sydney. About what my next venture will be. Her boyfriend also works for the magazine. It's absolutely nothing to do with *you*.' Her eyes flared, the green flecks sparking.

'But if she sees me—'

'You could stay in your room. Or leave early and spend the afternoon elsewhere. Go way out to sea with Wayan—'

'Why should I have to hide?'

She put up her hand in a halt sign. 'I haven't finished yet. I was going to say you *could* do all that but you don't need to do anything. Because the alternative is that I go in the morning to Sanur to the hotel where she's staying, for the interview and photo shoot. Then Maya will go over in the afternoon and we'll both stay in Sanur for a girls' night out with Sammie. I really want to see my friend. I haven't seen her for more than six months. But I don't want to put you out either. So that might be the best decision all round.'

In the face of her annoyance Max felt petty and mean. And gutted he wouldn't see her for all the time she was in Sanur. But the fear of media exposure of his affair with Nikki was still very real. Not that you could call it an affair yet. And the way she was glaring at him made him doubt an affair would ever eventuate.

Perhaps this would be a good opportunity to cool things down between him and Nikki before they ever really heated up. Before anyone—he was thinking of her—got hurt.

'You go to Sanur and do what you have to do. I hope the interview goes well for you.' He sincerely meant it.

'Thank you,' she said. 'It will be good PR for my new business. And for me. A positive feature should help re-establish my image as a serious businesswoman after the "runaway bride" scandal. Sammie has promised to completely avoid that term in her profile.'

'Good,' he said. 'Let's sit down and finish our meal.'

Nikki remained standing. 'Sorry. No can do.'

She stood there in a revealing pink bikini top with a hotel towel tucked around her waist, her feet bare, yet he could see her morphing into Nikki the businesswoman. Could almost see her thoughts veering away from him and towards her goals for the next day. 'I have to go,' she said, with what seemed to him to be only the merest trace of regret.

How could he have forgotten? Nikki Lucas was a high-powered businesswoman who had admitted to him she'd put dating on hold in favour of her work. She had been as driven to make her company a success as he'd been in his career as a sportsman. The odds of a young woman succeeding so spectacularly in the international market as she had were probably the same as of him winning the US Open.

'It's still early,' he said.

She shook her head. 'Not for all I have to do this evening. I have to call Sammie and tell her I've decided on the Sanur option. Let Maya know—Kadek will look after Putu for the night she's away but she might have to rearrange some staff shifts.'

'I get that, but it won't take long. Surely you don't need to go just yet.' Was he begging? Max swore under his breath. He never had, and never would, beg for a woman's company.

'Sadly I do,' she said. 'Because the shoot won't be happening here, I have to pack and take over stuff I might need in Sanur. I'll need to get an early boat, organise a hairdresser, then grab the opportunity to shop in boutiques in Sanur for a more businesslike outfit for the shoot than I brought with me when I came here. If we'd shot here, Sammie would have brought clothes with her for me but this way is better because I can choose my own outfit. I always like to have control of the image I present.'

'I was the same in my tennis career,' he said. Though in fact it had been his manager who had insisted on control over his image. Max had just wanted to play tennis. *To win.*

'Really? I suppose you would,' she said without any real interest.

The stiff set of her shoulders told him she was not happy with his reaction to her news about her friend's visit. But it wasn't just that. Her thoughts were racing away in a direction that led away from him. And Max wasn't sure he liked it.

CHAPTER ELEVEN

NIKKI HAD STRETCHED out her time in Sanur with her friends, delaying her return to Lembongan for as long as she could. Maya had left on the earliest boat in the morning. But it was late afternoon by the time the speedboat transporting Nikki back to the island was nearing the beach at Jungut Batu.

Nikki was oblivious to the beauty around her, the aquamarine waters, the tree-lined shore coming into view, the excited chatter of first-time visitors to the island. Despite the fun of seeing her friends, the challenge of the interview and photo shoot, she was too preoccupied.

She'd endured some emotional pain in her life, but few things had hurt like the shaft of pain that had stabbed her at Max's response to her thoughtless comment about sending him photos of desserts from the kitchens of Big Blue once he was back in Sydney. Of course she knew the score for a no-strings fling—don't expect anything more. Just walk away and pretend it doesn't hurt. But the obvious discomfort that had flickered across his face that she should dare to presume any ongoing contact with Max Conway, the celebrity sportsman, had made her cringe. Then his instant suspicion of her because she was seeing a friend who was a journalist—someone she'd known since they were fourteen years old—had driven the blade in deeper.

No more Max. She wasn't cut out for no-label flings, one-night stands, or whatever she chose to call them. He was a celebrity used, no doubt, to picking up and putting down women when it suited him. She, for all her business success, was just a girl who'd been wounded by the men she'd misjudged while looking for love and the not unreasonable expectation of marriage and a family. She wasn't good at pretending to be something else.

She liked Max. She liked him a lot. Thought he was the hottest man on the planet. But that closed-over look had told her she was in way above her head when it came to pretending she could easily cope with the aftermath of how she would feel when what Max was offering came to an end. She simply couldn't deal with it.

How could she endure these remaining nights with him on the island? She didn't want to let Maya down but she might have to decamp over to Sanur for the duration.

Not that Maya had expected her to stay as long as she had. They'd talked about that with Sammie on their girls' night out at a restaurant in Sanur. How Nikki had stretched her time on Lembongan for as long as she could—or should. That an exciting new venture awaited her, one that would continue her links with Maya and Frangipani Bay. But her life was in Sydney, not here. Sammie had asked her about her love life, concerned that she might not be getting over the Alan debacle. But Nikki had reassured her friend she was okay. Not ready to date okay, but okay just the same.

Neither Maya nor she had breathed a word to Sammie about Max being at Big Blue. Privately,

Maya had voiced her concern that Nikki might be heading for heartbreak. Which was perceptive of her as Nikki had not even confided in her how she felt about him. She had denied that she and Max were anything other than friends. But Maya's expression told her she knew better but wasn't going to interfere with further advice.

Perhaps, when it all boiled down to it, she should be thinking of flying back home rather than skulking in Sanur until Max checked out of Big Blue. Maybe she'd needed a kick in the butt like this to get back to face her real life.

Nevertheless, as she hitched up her dress above her knees to wade through the shallow water to the shore, it was with a heavy heart. Despite it all, she missed him. Every minute she'd been away from him, she had ached for him. There was something about her connection to Max that went beyond the physical, that called not only to her heart but to her soul.

Which was why she thought she might be hallucinating when she saw him standing on the beach, in the same place he'd stood when she'd last been here. She blinked. It was Max all right.

Tall, imposing. The same but different. Even more handsome, if that were possible. His beard was a proper short beard now, not the stubble of when she'd first seen him there. His shorts were grey not blue. And he was wearing the hat and sunglasses they'd agreed to wear in public.

Had he seen her? Could she turn around and take the speedboat back to the mainland? Panic tightened her throat. She wasn't ready for this. Had thought she'd have time to prepare herself before she spoke to him. *What was he doing here?*

He waved to her. There would be no escape. She would have to face him. But she wasn't going to be cowed by his presence.

'Mr James, what a coincidence,' she said lightly.

'It's no coincidence,' he said. 'Maya organised for the truck to come pick you up. I hitched a ride so I could meet you at the boat. I didn't want to hang around at the hotel waiting for you.'

She wasn't going to act all passive aggressive and angsty because he'd hurt her feelings. But she wasn't going to let the conversation get personal either. As far as she was concerned, their no-label fling had fizzled out. 'Thank you, but that wasn't necessary,' she said, forcing a polite smile. 'I trust our driver to get me back to Big Blue.' She knew she sounded stilted. But it was the best she could do. She screwed her eyes shut tight and wished he'd be gone when she opened them.

Nikki looked different, Max thought. Gone were the hippy pants, the tangle of windblown hair. Now her hair was sleek and sophisticated, falling below her shoulders; her eyes made up with some dark shadow; her mouth slicked a deep pink. Her natural-coloured linen dress looked elegant and businesslike, even with the flip-flops she'd worn for the boat. This wasn't his Nikki of the island or the Nikki of his dreams. Not that she'd ever been his, either in reality or dream.

He felt as if there were a sheet of glass between them. And it wasn't because she was wearing sunglasses and a hat and he couldn't properly see her expression.

He offered to carry her backpack for her but she demurred. 'It's nicely balanced,' she said.

'How did the interview go?' he asked as they walked to the waiting place for the truck. The streets were much too narrow for the driver to park anywhere and they had to wait for him to come back for them.

'Very well,' she said. 'Sammie asked some interesting questions, which really made me think.' She put up her hand as if to forestall a question from him. 'Rest assured, your name wasn't mentioned at all. The wedding incident was a no-go zone so you didn't even come up in reference to your role as best man. It was strictly business.'

'Good,' he said, relieved to hear it. He still worried at the wisdom of her meeting with a journalist. Journalists went for blood at the slightest sniff of a story, the more scandalous the better. And if it wasn't a scandal, they turned it into one—as he'd learned to his peril. If the press hadn't got hold of the paternity dispute story, it wouldn't have given his opponent the fuel to goad him into the ill-timed shot that had ended his career. He was glad he hadn't had to meet Sammie. It would have been difficult to be polite to her.

While he waited with Nikki for the truck they

made small talk about the hotel she had stayed at with her friends in Sanur. She was polite, pleasant, not a trace of snark in her voice or demeanour. But he realised she had not once met his gaze.

He'd blown it with her.

They sat on opposite benches on the back of the truck all the way back to the hotel. Max tried not to think of the last time they'd sat there together, Nikki with her blue dress slipping up her thighs, he trying not to stare too blatantly. Or to remember the previous night when his 'Nikki in her blue dress' dream had turned into a nightmare.

It had started as usual with her gliding up the aisle towards him, then lifting her face for his kiss. Only instead of kissing her, he'd watched as she'd turned away from him back to her groom. A groom who suddenly wasn't Alan but some anonymous dude gazing at her in adoration. The symbolism was painfully obvious—he couldn't give her what she wanted so she'd found someone else. In the dream the pain of his loss had seared through him. He'd awoken in a sweat and never returned to sleep, tossing and turning, thoughts and regrets churning through his brain.

He was beginning to realise that relationships were a fluid thing. Opportunities for something exciting and unexpected could slip away while he was trying to make everything perfect. There wasn't a perfect time for a relationship. You had to *make* the time. He might have good balance when it came to being nimble on his feet. What he didn't have was balance in his life. He *could* have both a career and a relationship. What appeared so patently obvious to others had been a revelation to him. Look how Maya and Kadek worked so harmoniously together—a business, a happy marriage, a child.

When it came to Nikki, it seemed he'd kept his eye off the ball and lost the game, forfeiting the prize that had been right under his nose.

Nikki looked unseeingly out of the truck as it bumped its way back to the hotel. Seeing Max, wanting him, was too difficult. It was impossible for her to stay in any kind of proximity to him. She would have to get right away from here, from Bali, from anywhere in Indonesia. Time to move on. Tonight she would get online and book a flight home. Many of the flights to Sydney left from the Ngurah Rai international airport in Denpasar very late in the evening so she would almost certainly be able to leave tomorrow. Maya would understand.

When they reached the hotel, Nikki accepted Max's offer of assistance with her backpack but not his hand to help her down from the truck. Not after what had happened last time. She flushed at the memory of that passionate, public kiss, furious at herself for the wave of longing for him that swept through her. Now Max kept at a polite distance but she was as aware of him as if they were skin-to-skin close. His scent, his warmth, the essence of his Max-ness. It was too painful. She had to go, and go quickly.

Packing up to leave Lembongan wouldn't take long. She hadn't brought much with her when she had fled Sydney and hadn't acquired much during her stay. Just the knick-knacks she'd bought to personalise her villa, a couple of gorgeous sarongs, this dress she'd bought for the interview.

Oh, and her heart. She'd been at risk of leaving that behind with the best man. It had been a close call.

She thanked the driver. He wasn't known to her, so she was very careful to stay staff-guest distance from Max and to address him as Mr James. But when the truck drove away from the driveway nearest to their villas she was left alone with Max. Most likely for the last time.

He refused to give her back her backpack, saying he would carry it to her villa for her. She walked the short distance to her door aware every second that he was only a few steps behind her. They reached her villa. He put her backpack down.

'Thank you,' she said. 'That was kind of you.' She went to fish in the outside pocket of it for her room key but her hands were shaking too much to make a connection. She closed her eyes in despair. This was dreadful. They'd been so at ease with each other. To be reduced to this level of awkwardness was unbearable.

'Let me,' he said, deftly retrieving her big old-fashioned key with the wooden tag and handing it to her. A gentleman to the last.

She took it, being ultra-careful their hands didn't brush in the process. 'Thank you,' she said again, in an excess of politeness to cover how she was crying in her heart that it had come to this. She feigned a yawn. 'I'm so tired, can't wait to get inside.' She'd been about to add *and out of this dress* but stopped herself in time.

'You left your uniform in my villa the other night,' he said. 'The top, the sash and the sarong.'

Nikki snatched her hand to her mouth. 'How careless of me. The housekeepers would have seen it and drawn their own conclusions.' She groaned. 'So much for being discreet.'

'They couldn't have seen it. I packed it away in my suitcase in my closet to keep it hidden until you came back.'

'Good idea,' she said. She would just leave the clothing there. Maya could retrieve it after she'd left.

'I could bring it out to you,' he said.

'That won't be necessary,' she said.

'Or you could come into my villa and get it,' he said.

'I… I don't think so.' She couldn't bear to be alone with him in the privacy of those high walls.

She looked up and finally caught his gaze, intensely blue in the fading light of the day. 'Please come in, Nikki,' he said. 'Please.'

CHAPTER TWELVE

NIKKI TOOK A deep breath to steady herself. Now would be as good a time as any to tell him she intended to fly back to Sydney tomorrow evening. After all, he hadn't actually done anything wrong. She had simply decided not to accept the terms he was offering. Her choice. They should part on civilised terms.

Mutely, she nodded.

She followed him through the courtyard and into his villa. He closed the door and stood with it behind him, facing her. 'I missed you, Nikki. Every minute you were away I missed you. This place was so empty without you. I know you were angry with me. I was—'

Her carefully rehearsed explanation of why she was going fled from her mind. 'I missed you too,' she said, something she had had no intention of admitting. 'Every second I wished you were with me. I couldn't sleep for thinking about you. Yearning for you. But I can't do a no-strings fling, Max. And I actually don't see at this stage what's stopping us from treating this like a normal boy-meets-girl scenario. Okay, so we want to avoid media intrusion, keep things private. We're on the same page there.'

'Yes,' he said vehemently with a curse that told her exactly what he thought of the media.

'But we're both single. Free to see whoever we want. We've both been burned before in other relationships. I… I'm scared of getting hurt again. I admit I have trust issues. But I also really enjoy being with you. More than any other man I've ever met. A few days here has established that. If we like each other why—?'

'Can't we just date and see where it leads to?'

'I was going to say why hedge ourselves with restrictions like one night but you said it better. I deserve better than to be seen as a no-strings fling to be picked up then discarded. And so do you.'

He looked at her quizzically. 'That's not the

kind of thing a girl usually says to a guy. That he deserves more than a passing encounter.'

'I mean it. But if you still don't think you can fit a meaningful relationship into your new life after tennis, then say goodbye for good now.'

Their gazes held for a long moment. The hunger she saw in his eyes was surely reflected in hers. She swayed towards him. All thoughts fled her mind except how much she wanted him. *Max.*

'I don't want to say goodbye,' he said.

He kissed her and she kissed him back without hesitation. They skipped the tender, questing kind of warm-up kiss and went straight to demanding and urgent. He bunched her hair in his hand and tugged to tilt her face upward to deepen the kiss. The tug on her hair should have hurt but it didn't. It thrilled her. *He* thrilled her.

Pent-up desire ignited and flamed through her. He pulled away from the kiss, to say something, she thought. But there had been enough words. She pressed her mouth back against his to silence him, slipped her tongue between his lips, demanded more. She slid her arms under his shirt, around his waist to hold warm, bare skin. He slid his hands down her shoulders past the curves of her breasts to hold her bottom. Her nipples tightened and tingled and she pressed her body close to his. Close, closer, not close enough. *She wanted more.*

She murmured deep in her throat. Pleasure, want, hunger. He groaned and held her closer. She stepped back, trying to drag him in the direction of the bedroom but she met an immovable wall of muscle. Then he propelled her forward. Then they were stumbling towards his bedroom, laughing when they bumped into the wall and knocked a wooden carving askew, laughing when they got tangled up in the mosquito net, laughing when they met a recalcitrant zipper or tore off a button in their haste to strip each other of their clothes.

'This would be so much easier if we were wearing sarongs,' she murmured in mock complaint.

'Or a towel and a pink bikini,' he said.

Then their laughter slowed to murmurs and sighs and moans as they explored each other's wants and needs.

* * *

Nikki woke up and thought for a moment she was in her own bed in her own villa. The bed was identical. Same mosquito-net canopy. Same ceiling fan with cane blades flicking languorously around. What was different was the warm male body next to her, hand resting possessively on her thigh. Max. *Her lover.*

And what an awesome lover he was. Passionate, energetic, inventive. Not to mention thoughtful and considerate. They had seemed to instinctively know what pleased each other. After their first time together, they had fallen asleep in each other's arms. It was dark when they'd woken, ravenous, and ordered pizza from room service. *Nasi goreng* didn't seem quite the thing to eat in bed.

He'd then fulfilled all her built-up fantasies of him—and she his—in his open-air bathroom as they'd showered together. When they eventually fell asleep again it was the deep sleep of the totally exhausted.

Now shafts of sunlight were filtering through the blinds, picking up the gold in Max's beard, the fine hair on his chest and legs. Heaven knew what time it was.

She stretched out her satisfied, pleasurably aching body. Max lay asleep on his back beside her, his limbs sprawled across the bed in the same confident possession of space that had become so familiar. His hand stayed on her thigh and she tentatively covered it with hers.

She didn't think she had ever felt happier. She wanted this. Wanted *him*. There was no use in denying it any further. *She was falling in love with him.*

The first thing Max saw when he woke was Nikki smiling into his face. She lay next to him, her head turned to his. With her hair dishevelled and spread across the pillow, dark smudges of make-up under her eyes, her lips swollen from his kisses, she had never looked more beautiful. She was naked and unselfconscious, her lovely body gilded with sunlight.

He noted with a stab of guilt slight marks from his fingers on the smooth skin of her thighs. But he remembered when he'd given them to her and

she hadn't been complaining. A fierce posses-
siveness surged through him. She was perfect in
every way. *She was his.*

'Hey, you,' he said, dropping a kiss on her
mouth.

'Hey to you too,' she said, nipping on his lower
lip.

'This is nice,' he said, knowing the words were
grossly inadequate to express how he felt.

'Yes,' she said, and he knew he didn't need the
words. 'Do I wish we'd done this the first night
we knew we wanted to do it?'

'Do you?'

'No. It wouldn't have been the same.'

'I think I could have been okay with it that first
night,' he said. In fact he knew so. He had wanted
her from the get-go. 'But I want more.'

'Now?' she said, wiggling closer to him.

He stroked the fine strands of her hair back
from where they were falling across her face.
'Yes,' he said, immediately ready for her. 'But
what I meant was I want this to continue. Us, I
mean.' He laughed. 'I'm not very good at this.

If I was sixteen I'd say I want you to be my girl-friend.'

'That's not a bad way of putting it even for a thirty-year-old,' she said. 'I know exactly what you mean. I'd like to be your girlfriend.' She stroked his face with delicate fingers from his cheekbone to the corner of his mouth. 'Very much so.'

'I want to enjoy all the time we can have together here and then afterwards. What are your plans? I could try to get up here as often as possible, but it would be easier if we were in the same city. Sydney, I mean. For the foreseeable future anyway.' If he took the sports announcer job he could be based anywhere. But rather than thinking he had to make those decisions on his own, he realised with a surprising sense of relief he might make them with Nikki. Make a decision based on what she wanted as well as his own needs.

'I was talking about that with my friends last night,' she said. 'Me moving back to Sydney, I mean. Going back to my old life.' Her voice trailed away and he realised she was still nervous about going home.

'Not quite the same old life with a new boy-friend,' he said.

Her eyes brightened. The way the green seemed to appear among the brown at different times continued to fascinate him. 'What an exceedingly appealing thought,' she said, her lips curving into a luminescent smile. 'That makes me much happier about going home—sooner rather than later.'

'Good,' he said. Later he might broach the subject of her coming back on the same flight as him. That and the other vexed topic of how they would handle being seen together in the public eye. Perhaps he could talk to his publicist about making a media announcement, keeping the public perception of his relationship with Nikki under his control.

But right now she was snuggling close to him and pressing a trail of little kisses across his chest and up towards his mouth. Thoughts of an entirely different nature took over and he rolled Nikki over so he could kiss her back. She wound her arms around his neck and whispered exactly what she'd like to do to him. Who was he to resist?

CHAPTER THIRTEEN

WHEN NIKKI NEXT woke, the sun was seriously bright in Max's bedroom and her mobile phone was vibrating all over the bedside table. Blearily she reached out to get it, blinked herself awake when she noticed the number of messages, both voicemail and text, that had come in.

Alarmed, she sat up in bed, now wide awake. Was something wrong back home?

She opened the urgent text from her sister.

Nikki, you need to look at this. Then call me.

With fingers that were suddenly unsteady, Nikki clicked on the link to the website of a popular tabloid newspaper. The words screamed up at her: *'Runaway bride and traitor best man enjoy raunchy romp in tropical love nest!'*

For a shocked second she thought it was a rehash of the 'secret Fiji love nest' beat-up that had run six months ago. Then she focussed on the photos that ran below the headline. And had to swallow against the nausea that rose in her throat.

The photos had been taken here on this island. Recently. The main shot was a zoomed-in image of her and Max kissing in the laneway outside the sunset restaurant, her blue dress rucked up and exposing an indecent amount of bare thigh as well as bare back. The kiss was hungry and passionate—as indeed it had been. But the way the image had been cropped made it look seedy.

The next one was another of her with Max, their heads very close together, smiling intimately at each other at the restaurant table. They looked like lovers. In fact it was captioned *'The Look of Love?'* Under any other circumstance Nikki would think it beautiful and want a copy.

The final shot was of her and Max, shoulders touching, wading out of the water together at Frangipani Bay, she in her high-cut red swimsuit and the tight black swim shirt that, when wet, revealed every curve and indent of her body. Max was wearing just his black swim shorts, the rest of his magnificent body bare and glistening with drops of water. She was laughing up at him as if she was besotted. That one was captioned *'Hot Stuff!'*

And of course, under those photos, there was an old one of Max running away from the church, carrying her in his arms.

Other captions referred to Max's tennis career: *'Tennis star not too injured to enjoy sexy tryst with friend's fiancée!'* was the only one she could bear to read.

She closed her eyes but it was all there in front of her when she opened them again and she was plunged back into the nightmare she'd thought she'd left behind. *Dear heaven, how had this happened?*

She scrolled down her messages. They were from other friends alerting her to the article. Reporters asking for comments. Her father demanding to know what the hell was going on.

She gagged as she forced herself to read through the rest of the story, under the byline of *'Our reporter on Lembongan Island'*. She and Max had let themselves believe they'd had privacy in this out-of-the-way place. How naive they'd been.

Beside her, Max stirred. Looking over to his side of the bed, she could see his phone was flashing with messages too.

He opened his eyes. Smiled at her as if it was the happiest thing ever for him to find her there in his bed. But her expression must have told him something was wrong. He sat up. 'You okay?' he asked, wary.

Nikki shook her head, fighting tears. She wanted to scream and cry and shout. But she managed a choked, 'Not okay.' Without another word, she handed him over her phone open at the offending article.

'Why have the bridesmaid when the best man snagged the bride?' was another headline.

Oh, it was awful. What was beautiful between them was now being made to look sleazy. But at least this time they could face the media united as a couple.

Max's face darkened as he read. He cursed. Threw her phone on the bed. Then scowled. 'Your friend Sammie.' He spat out the words.

'Some friend she is. How did you let this happen, Nikki? I thought you said you could trust her.'

'You think this is Sammie? This isn't her. She's not that type of journalist. It's some tourist with a smartphone. Everyone is a paparazzi these days. He—the photo credit is a he, probably a fake name—most likely recognised you then realised who I must be. Then he's stalked us. Taken the opportunity to make some cash to fund his vacation by selling the photos to the trashy tabloid. They've then got some desk hack to cobble together an article.'

She picked up her phone from where Max had thrown it and scrolled through some more. 'Thank heaven he didn't get behind our courtyard walls.'

Max glared at her. 'Only because I stopped your friend from coming over here.'

'That's ridiculous,' she said.

Nikki pulled the sheet up over her breasts. Felt uncomfortable in front of him now when she'd been so uninhibited all night.

'Is it? You shouldn't have talked to a journalist, Nikki.'

She gritted her teeth. 'This has got nothing to do with me talking to Sammie.'

'She could have shared her information with a mate on the tabloid. These photos were taken with a long-distance lens. A professional camera.'

'Smartphones can have adjustable lenses. I'm telling you this is an opportunistic amateur trying to make a tidy sum from invading our privacy.'

Max swung his legs over and sat on the edge of the bed, his bare back to her. He muttered an inventive string of curses. 'You'd better get back to your own villa now this has hit the fan.'

'What? You're kicking me out?'

He turned to her. 'We don't want your "opportunistic tourist" seeing us like this.' He cursed again. 'Don't you see how bad this is? Last time, the media could lie all it liked but I knew the truth. I had behaved with honour. Now it looks like I ran away with you for a quick—'

'Don't say it. That disrespects me. And you. How do you think I feel about this? It's always worse for the woman. My father will be spitting. My sister is upset too.'

'My parents won't like it either. They wouldn't

see this as honourable behaviour. Even though my father didn't particularly like Alan when we played tennis together all those years ago.'

'Actually it was an honourable thing you did by helping me escape what would almost certainly have been a disastrous marriage. This interest in us is only because you're a celebrity. You're news. I'm not. *Any* female "frolicking" with Max Conway would be news.'

'The way you look in the red swimsuit makes you news,' he said through obviously gritted teeth. 'And good publicity for your swim school.'

'Are you serious? You can't mean that?'

'Of course not,' he muttered. But she was shocked he could even think it.

'Max, can I be the voice of reason here? This is awful. I'm not saying it's anything less than despicable that these people have tried to drag our names through the mud. But we actually haven't done anything wrong. Nothing underhand or sordid. The wedding was six months ago. Alan has moved on to more profitable pastures. So we met when you helped me run away? Big deal. Isn't that what the movies call "a cute meet"?' The stubborn set of his face told her she wasn't getting through to him. 'Viewed through a different lens, I might have thought the way we met and then reconnected by accident on this beautiful island was...was romantic.'

He picked up his phone and groaned. 'There's nothing vaguely romantic about *"Tennis star not too injured to enjoy sexy tryst with friend's fiancée!"'*

With what seemed to Nikki like morbid interest, Max continued to scroll through the story. 'The comments from readers are even worse.' He cradled his head in his hands.

'Well, don't read them,' she said. 'I didn't.'

He didn't seem to notice when she tiptoed around the bed, still wrapped in the sheet, to retrieve her dress, then her panties and bra from where Max had tossed them on the floor last night.

She ran into the bathroom with her clothes clutched to her front. Quickly she slipped into her underwear, then pulled her crumpled linen dress on over her head. She wet a tissue and wiped away the worst of her mascara panda eyes. Then dragged Max's comb through her hair. Her worst fear—one she didn't dare share with Max—was that there would be photographers waiting outside Max's villa hoping to catch her leaving in a morning-after-the-night-before 'walk of shame'. As Sydney was two hours ahead of Lembongan in time difference, and the news mightn't have hit here yet, she might be lucky.

Max barred her way at the doorway from the bedroom. Standing there stark naked, he looked so magnificent she had to force herself not to stare. Not to take him by the hand and lead him back to the bed. But she was beginning to doubt whether she actually wanted to be his girlfriend. A good relationship needed more than good sex. Like trust. Particularly trust.

'Where are you going?'

'You told me to get next door and so I am.'

If he let her slink out there by herself without him by her side to support her, it was over.

'I'm not sure that's a good idea,' he said. 'There might be more of those leeches out there.'

She glared at him. 'Max, what's wrong with

this picture? We should be dealing with this to-gether. Instead you're blaming me.'

'I didn't say that.'

'You're refusing to believe I didn't slip an ex-clusive to my journalist friend.'

'You must admit the timing of her visit is sus-picious.'

'We went to that sunset restaurant on Thurs-day evening. She and her boyfriend didn't fly into Bali until Friday afternoon. She, or her boy-friend, couldn't possibly have taken those pho-tos. Besides, she writes serious stuff for quality media, not tabloid rubbish. It might have been someone in that group of people who brushed past us in the laneway. It could have been any-one with a smartphone.'

He brandished his phone. 'There's a lot of good publicity for Big Blue in this article. According to it, the resort is a perfect place for a "raunchy romp".'

'As it turned out, it actually was perfect for that purpose.' She caught his eye. If he laughed she'd give him more credit on his trust account. He didn't laugh. 'But surely you're not pinning any of this on Maya or Kadek?'

He paused for a second too long. 'Of course not.'

She screwed up her face in what she hoped he would recognise as a look of loathing. 'Not in a million years would they do this to me.' Not content with calling her, in not so many words, a liar, now he was casting slurs on the honesty of the most scrupulously honest people she knew. He was right back there with the wounding words, one stab for her and two more on behalf of her friends.

'Not them, but perhaps someone on the staff.'

'I didn't realise you were so stubborn,' she said. 'We're victims here, me as much as you.'

'Tenacious is how my game was described,' he said. 'I won't give up until I find out who did this to us.'

Did this to *you*, she thought. He didn't seem to give a damn about the effect on her. She was surprised to realise how self-centred Max was. How gutted she was to realise it. When she thought back to it, this…this *affair*—because she now realised that was all it was—had been all about him. His need for privacy, his need to re-establish himself. He hadn't uttered one word of comfort to her. All she wanted was for him to take her in his arms and tell her they were in this together and he was by her side. *Wasn't going to happen.*

'I told you trust is important to me. You don't believe I'm telling the truth. Can you imagine how painful it is for me to be considered a liar? You don't trust me. And I can't trust you to support me. You deal with this in your own way. I'll deal with it in mine.'

She marched to the door outside to the courtyard. Hoped he might follow her. Realised that would be impossible as he didn't have a stitch on. If there was indeed a photographer lurking, Max Conway naked after 'lusty night with busty blonde' would be the money shot of that photographer's career.

She couldn't look back. If she managed to get on a plane tonight that might be the last time she saw Max and she didn't want him to see the tears that she could no longer stop from cascading down her cheeks. Once again she had totally misjudged the true character of a man she had fallen for. She was disappointed in herself as much as him. She'd really thought he was everything she wanted.

CHAPTER FOURTEEN

MAX IMMEDIATELY REALISED he had made one of
the worst mistakes of his life. Nikki had hit him
with the news of the latest media outrage as he'd
woken up from a new and improved version of
the 'Nikki in the blue dress' dream. Nikki had
been in the church wearing the blue dress but
not for a wedding rehearsal. She'd been holding a baby in her arms and they were there for
a christening. At first it was black-haired baby
Putu with Nikki but then, in the way of dreams,
the baby morphed into a blond-haired baby that
looked just like Max's baby photos. His baby.

His and Nikki's baby.

In his dream, she'd held their baby out to him
and he'd been overjoyed, which was odd as he
wasn't at all comfortable with holding babies.
That was probably why he woke up. But he'd

been only half awake. Awake enough to register the joy of finding Nikki naked in his bed, asleep enough to be about to murmur, *Did we have a boy or a girl?* Then her real-life expression had alerted him to the fact that something was very wrong.

He'd overreacted big-time to what he'd seen on her phone. Thinking on his feet had stood him in good stead on the tennis court. But it had let him down badly here. Worse, he'd been unable to let go of the idea that Nikki had somehow contributed to the disaster through her journalist friend, Sammie. He'd just looked Sammie up to find what Nikki had said was true. She was a serious, award-winning journalist. Not only would she be unlikely to stoop to tabloid trash, he doubted she'd betray her friend. Nikki inspired loyalty from a group of long-term friends. He, having just asked her to be his girlfriend, had been guilty of stunning disloyalty in not believing her and supporting her. He'd virtually called her a liar.

Fact was, he'd been so determined to pin down the nearest scapegoat, because he knew who was really at fault. Him. As soon as he'd seen that photo of him kissing Nikki in that laneway he'd known the whole disaster had been because of him. In spite of his past history with the tabloids he had been so enchanted with her he'd let down his guard. He had given in to the impulse to kiss her in that laneway even though there had been people about. And as such, he'd failed to protect her. It was that photo that had led to the others. To some creep stalking his lovely Nikki.

The other fact was he simply was not used to thinking as a couple. What had Ellen accused him of being? *'Max first, Max last, and Max in between.'* That might have been true then, when his entire focus had been on his game. But it shouldn't be now. He'd gone into his default protect-his-reputation-at-all-costs mode as soon as he'd seen those scurrilous headlines—so like the headlines that had plagued him before. It was like when he'd got completely immersed in 'the zone' before a game. No one could reach him once he'd reached that state.

But he wasn't playing competitive tennis any more. He'd zoned out and been impervious to the common-sense explanations that Nikki had repeatedly tried to get him to accept. Worse, he had hurt her. Hurt the woman he had realised was vital to his future happiness. Possibly scuppered his chances to make any kind of life with her.

He had to find her. Apologise. Explain. Make amends.

He quickly showered and headed next door. She wasn't there. Or was refusing to acknowledge him. He sounded the chimes. Shouted into the intercom. Even gave an impatient kick to the heavy carved wooden door. Which wasn't a good idea when he was wearing flip-flops.

Kadek approached from the boardwalk just in time to see him kick the door. 'Sorry, Kadek, I'll pay for any damage,' Max said immediately.

Kadek looked amused. 'You're more likely to damage your foot than that door,' he said. Max could hardly look the guy in the eye. Kadek had invited him to dinner at his house the night Nikki had stayed in Sanur. And in return he had included him in his list of suspects. He had a lot of amends to make.

'If you're looking for Nikki, I saw her heading down to the beach. She said she was taking a kayak out.' Thankfully Kadek didn't mention any media reports. He'd see them soon enough, if he hadn't already. Something good might come of it if it helped put Big Blue more on the map for potential guests.

Wayan was on the beach when Max got there. He confirmed Nikki had taken out a kayak. Even though he had warned her that the currents might be unpredictable today. He pointed out to Max where she'd gone.

Shading his eyes against the sun, Max could see Nikki in her red swim shirt and yellow life jacket paddling to the headland at the south end of the beach. *What the hell was she doing?* Around that headland were wild surf beaches, including the beach at the sunset restaurant. He recalled with a shudder how those waves had pounded against the limestone cliffs. Even in a special surf kayak it would be highly dangerous.

Nikki. She seemed very small in a very big sea out there by herself. As he watched, she disappeared out of sight around the headland.

Max ran to Wayan. 'Let me have your boat,' he said.

Within minutes he was heading out after Nikki in Wayan's *jukung*. As he neared the headland the currents came at him from all directions, buffeting the boat. Nobody should be in a kayak in these waters. Fear gripped his gut.

He gunned the motor. The boat surged through the water. He had to get to her. Had to make sure she was safe. Had to tell her…had to tell her so many things. How sorry he was. How much he regretted the way he'd behaved, not just this morning, but since he'd been on the island. How he'd let his loathing of the media make him hide her, as if she were some guilty secret, instead of shouting to the world how lucky he was to have this beautiful, perfect woman in his life. How blind he'd been to place her behind his career plans instead of putting her first. First in *everything*. Most of all he had to tell her how much— Max stopped his crazy flow of thoughts as the truth hit him harder that the most powerful wave. *How much he loved her.*

Love. He'd tried to deny to himself that he had fallen in love with her. But he'd been kidding himself from the word go. He'd fallen a little in love with her as far back as her wedding re-hearsal. That was another reason he'd overreacted to the media interest in them. Deep down, when he'd helped her run away from her wedding, hadn't part of his heart wished he were running away with her for himself?

That was what all the dreams had been telling him—his subconscious shouting out to him what his conscious mind refused to acknowledge. *He loved Nikki Lucas.*

He rounded the first headland, scanning the water for her. Nothing. Not even other small craft. Sensible people did not go out in this kind of current. Why had Nikki?

The current got stronger, the water choppier; he had to fight with the steering wheel to keep the boat on course as he rounded the next set of jagged cliffs.

He saw the oar first. A lone paddle floating on the surface, pulled inextricably by the water towards where it would be smashed against the rocks. So close it wasn't safe for him to retrieve it. In the next split second he saw Nikki. Lying draped across the hull of her capsized kayak.

She was very, very still. Injured? Unconscious? Worse? *No!*

He hit the gas so hard the boat reared up out of the water. 'Nikki!' he shouted, the word reverberating around the empty sea.

As he neared her, she lifted her head. 'Max. Thank heaven,' she gasped. Her face was pale, which made the blood trickling down her mouth seem shockingly red in contrast.

He manoeuvred the boat as close as he could get to her. Fear strangled his voice. 'I'm coming for you,' he choked out.

'The kayak capsized. I tried to grab the hull to pull it back over to me, like I've done a hundred times before.' A choppy wave broke over the kayak, pushed it forward and splashed into her face, sending her sliding back into the sea. 'Aargh!' she spluttered. 'But that keeps happening.'

His first instinct was to dive overboard and get her. But that would leave them both bobbing in the ocean while Wayan's boat drifted away. 'Grab the outrigger,' he said as he manoeuvred the boat closer.

Nikki was an excellent swimmer. She was wearing a life jacket but she was bleeding. His gut roiled as he watched her wait for a lull in the choppy sea and then push herself forward until she was gripping the outrigger. He reached out to haul her in but she was just out of reach. He cursed. Then remembered the ladder. He quickly put it in place. 'Swim to the ladder,' he urged her.

Then he had her in his grasp as he pulled her on board. She was in his arms, wet, shaking, *alive*. He guided her onto the bench, where he sat next to her. 'You're bleeding,' he said, wiping the blood away from her chin.

'Am I?' she said, putting her hand up to her face. 'Oh. That. Bumped my nose. It's nothing. I'm fine.'

'Nothing!' Anger surged through his relief. 'I thought you'd drowned. What the hell were you thinking, coming out here by yourself? How many times did you warn me against it? Don't you ever do something so foolish again.'

Nikki stiffened and shuffled herself along the bench as far away from him as she could without toppling back into the water. As he manoeuvred the boat away from the rocks and back towards the shore, he realised with a chill that went right through to his heart that she wasn't just putting a physical distance between them.

'I'm glad you came along,' she said finally after what felt like hours of silence. They were nearly at the beach when she continued, 'Appreciate the help. But I don't owe you an explanation. Not as your ex-girlfriend of less than twenty-four hours' standing.'

'You're my ex-girlfriend before you've even had time to be my girlfriend?'

'Why would I want to be the girlfriend of a guy who calls me a liar, who refuses to listen to me, who can't act as a boyfriend-girlfriend team, who kicks me out of his room after we'd spent the night making love?'

As he hauled the boat onto the deserted beach, he moored it, finally turning to help her out of the boat. Her eyes were red-rimmed, her face splotchy. Not just with salt water. She'd been crying, crying for some time. Her words were tough but he could see the deep level of pain in her eyes. *He'd hurt her badly.* That was why she'd gone out there by herself. To get as far away from him as possible. *He'd lost her.*

But Max Conway didn't easily accept defeat. He waited until she stood beside him on the sand before finding the words he needed to say.

'Nikki, I'm sorry. You're right. I'm a rotten boyfriend who doesn't deserve you. I've been an idiot. Not just this morning but since the day I watched you step off that boat at Jungut Batu and wade back into my life. For too many stupid reasons I've handled this so badly.'

'Handled what, Max?' she said, her chin still held at a mutinous angle but her expression softened into wary anticipation.

'The fact I'm head over heels in love with you. That nothing else matters but that I'm with you. Not career, not reputation, nothing. That I fell in love with you that first night at the rehearsal of your wedding to another man. I had to deny it then. But I don't have to deny it now. I love you, Nikki.'

Nikki wondered if she'd been knocked unconscious by the edge of the kayak and was hallucinating. Perhaps she was still drifting along in that glorious sea, dreaming of what she wanted most in the world. That Max loved her.

Then she felt the touch of his hand on her arm. Saw the trepidation in his eyes as he waited for her response. *Max loved her.*

'Is there a chance you might love me too?' he said. 'Or is it only about the hot sex for you?'

Her joyous laughter pealed out across the empty beach. 'I love you too, Max.' He kissed her, warm and passionate and tender and *loving* all at the same time. 'And I love the hot sex too,' she murmured against his mouth. They kissed for a long time, each repeating those magical words 'I love you' with increasing wonderment and joy.

'When—?'

'Did I first fall in love with you?' she said. 'I realised I was attracted to you when you carried me away in your arms at the wedding. But here, on this island, on this sea, exploring the underwater paradise together, I realised it was so much more than that. When you kissed me at sunset I knew I was in love.'

'We wasted so much time,' he said.

'Only a few days, though it seems longer,' she said. 'Can we truly fall in love so quickly?'

He smiled. 'Thirty-two years ago my father spotted my mother across the hall at a country dance. He was smitten. Fortunately so was she. They married three months later and are still the happiest couple I know.'

Her breath caught. 'Do you take after your dad?'

'Definitely. I don't need more time. Will you marry me, Nikki?'

Her heart seemed to swell with her love for him. 'Yes, Max, yes.'

'I want to give you everything you want, Nikki. Marriage, children when you're ready. Most of all a husband you can trust to love you and care for you for the rest of our lives.'

'All I want is you,' she murmured through a suddenly constricted throat. 'Everything else will be a bonus.'

He kissed her again for a long time. She couldn't think of a more perfect proposal on the beautiful empty beach, with the vastness of the ocean stretched out before them, in this magical place where they'd each found their for ever love. That they were both wearing life jackets was something to tell the grandchildren.

He broke away from the kiss. 'Instead of hiding us from the media, I should have taken out an advert in that dreadful tabloid and screamed it out in tall black headlines: *"Best Man Loves Runaway Bride."* Only now I'd add, *"And Makes Her His Wife".*'

She laughed. 'Sounds like a plan,' she said, as she drew him to her for another kiss.

CHAPTER FIFTEEN

Three months later, Nusa Lembongan

THIS WEDDING WASN'T strictly their wedding. Nikki and Max had discovered it was legally more straightforward to actually get married in Australia and have the wedding blessed in Indonesia. But this was the place they'd fallen in love and the place they wanted to make a public declaration of their commitment to each other. With a big party to celebrate.

In Sydney, Nikki and Max had got married in the tiny chapel at her old school with just a handful of guests comprising family and their very closest friends, including Max's mother and father, who Nikki already adored. She'd had just her sister Kaylie as bridesmaid and Max's brother had been best man. Her father had given her away and she'd been surprised to see him shed a tear as he'd told her how much he wished her mother could have been here for her special day.

Now here she and Max were on the beach at Frangipani Bay under an arch covered with frangipani and gold-painted ceremonial flowers. She wore a long, white dress trimmed with handmade lace, her feet bare in the sand. Max wore white trousers and shirt, his feet bare too. Kaylie was bridesmaid again, along with Maya and Sammie.

The entire resort had been booked out for the guests they had flown up to the island. They included staff members from the residential tennis training college Max had started to give talented kids from underprivileged backgrounds the same opportunities to excel that he'd had. He'd told Nikki he was enjoying his involvement with it more than he could have imagined. But he got a different kind of satisfaction from his directorship of the sporting goods company. He had a team working on the swimwear for Nikki's first swim club, which was nearly ready to open its doors—already there'd been a lot of interest and advance bookings.

The wedding was being covered by the same

classy magazine that had published the feature on Nikki and Max's romance to set their story straight, from the 'cute meet' as runaway bride and the best man, to the happy coincidence of their meeting again six months later on the island.

As they joyously repeated their vows, Max kept Nikki's hand firmly held in his. 'There's no way you're running away from this wedding,' he said.

'Why would I,' she said, looking up to his beloved face, 'when I'm already married to the best man?'

* * * * *

LET'S TALK

For exclusive extracts, competitions and special offers, find us online:

f facebook.com/millsandboon

○ @millsandboonuk

ꚛ @millsandboon

Or get in touch on 0844 844 1351*

For all the latest titles coming soon, visit millsandboon.co.uk/nextmonth